I0728360

DAVID NETH

FUSE

OBLIVION

BOOK 3

DN Publishing

Oblivion
Fuse, Book 3
Copyright © 2018 by David Neth
Batavia, NY

www.DavidNethBooks.com

Publisher: David Neth
Editing: Amy Maddox of The Blue Pencil
Proofreading: John Ognibene

ISBN: 978-1-945336-72-0
First edition

Subscribe to the author's newsletter for updates and exclusive content:
DavidNethBooks.com/Newsletter

Follow the author at:
www.facebook.com/DavidNethBooks
www.twitter.com/DavidNethBooks
www.instagram.com/dneth13

Also by David Neth

Fuse Series
Origin

Omertà

Small Town Christmas Series
A Christmas Reunion

Under the Moon Series
The Full Moon

The Harvest Moon

The Blood Moon

The Crescent Moon

The Blue Moon

The Art of Magic

Anthology
Collateral Damage:
A Superhero Anthology

Short Stories
Limelight

Snow After Christmas

Nonfiction
Go Indie: A Guide to Your First
Year Self-Publishing

Chapter One

I can see my breath in the early-March cold. I'm tucked inside the shadow of the old water pump station by the lake in my mostly black Fuse suit. My breath is about the only part of me that can be seen.

Dean, however, who's on my right, is easier to spot. Despite his best efforts to remain inconspicuous in his black hoodie and dark jeans, he still stands out in the moonlight. Wes has offered to make him a suit like mine, but Dean straight-up refuses. I guess I can't blame him. As much as my suit has helped me, it has a tendency of riding up.

Looking down the hill covered in weeds, I have a clear view of the water and the dock leading to a gravel lot. A narrow stone path leads up to the city streets, but for the most part, this area has been forgotten.

We were going to head to the Works, like we've been doing almost every night since my brother, Cale, disappeared four months ago, but we heard on the police scanner that the security system at the old city pump house went off. The police deemed the trigger to be faulty wiring in an old building. It still sounded suspicious to us, so we decided to check it out.

Based off images we pulled from the nearby rail yard security cameras before we came, there are five men down here. We ran the images through the facial recognition software I created and, no surprise, they're criminals. Even if it doesn't provide us any new information on Cale—which, if it follows every other lead we've chased down, it won't—it's something Fuse needs to take care of. Still, I'd rather not be shot by a couple of street thugs.

Dean pulls out the magazine from his gun and checks the ammunition. Again. With all the movement he makes—not to mention the clicking of his gun every time he opens it—we're just increasing our chances of being spotted. I look over at Dean's fidgeting hands and then up at him. Even though he can't see my face through my mask, he gets the message.

"Sorry," he mutters.

Turning my attention back down the hill, I watch as a couple of stray cats bow their heads to a puddle and start lapping up the water. In the distance, a small boat cuts through the stillness of the water.

Tonight's outing is more or less the same thing we've done every night since Cale disappeared. We've followed up on a lot of leads, except the most obvious one: Leon Wallace and Carlo Martelli. In other words, Dean's father and his friend. We haven't broached that option simply because it's such a delicate topic. How do you investigate a mob boss without giving away the fact that he's being investigated? And it's not just Martelli and Wallace I need to be careful with, it's also the police and Dean's feelings on the matter that I need to dance around carefully.

I lean back against the brick wall of the pump station and look up. The lights from the city are too bright to spot any stars, so I can't really see anything, but I need a minute to rest my eyes.

Dean nudges me and points out to the lake. The small speedboat is almost to shore. Although nobody runs out to the docks to greet it, I know those five men from the cameras are probably still here, just waiting to receive whatever it is that's on the boat.

Our coms have been tuned in to the police scanners, listening for anything out of the ordinary. There hasn't been any mention of the pump station since the police deemed it unimportant, but with the Martelli crime family running the city and the rogue Michael Bello collecting his own forces, it's best to take precaution. The continued gang violence in the Hopman neighborhood are proof that Michael Bello is building up his forces. This was the area he covered when he was one of Martelli's capos. Problem is, we haven't actually laid eyes on him since he was arrested back in November.

As the boat approaches the dock, two men from one of the warehouses near the shore run out to help pull it in. The light down here is minimal because it's mostly an abandoned dock that's surrounded by the rail yard, so we can just barely make out the men's movements from this far away. We need to get closer.

"Ready?" I ask.

Dean holds out his arm in front of me. "Wait. For all we know, this could be a legitimate thing. Maybe it's not illegal. Let's wait it out a little more."

I doubt it. I suspect he agrees with me, but it's still better to cover our bases. Yet another example that even though I've been Fuse for several months now, I'm still learning not to be hasty.

We watch as the other three men also run out to the dock and begin unloading big black boxes from the boat. While one trudges up the stone walkway to the warehouse, the second guy sets down his box and pulls out something large. As he moves out of the shadows, I see it's a semiautomatic rifle.

The third guys points to the bin, yanks the gun out of the second one's hands, and replaces it in the box before hauling it up the path with a fourth guy. The first guy passes them on his way to the boat for another box.

"Still think it's legitimate?" I ask Dean.

He rolls his eyes. "Be ready with your mojo. We still need to get closer before we attack."

We're fifty feet away from the dock and we have no idea whether those guns are loaded. If we give away our location too soon, they could open fire on us and we'd be dead.

Keeping low, I lead Dean through the underbrush near the

water, dropping to the ground when they look our way. Only twenty-five feet away now.

"Wait until they're away from the boat," Dean mutters through the com in my ear.

I give a slight nod and look back to the men. Two of them are on the boat and the other three are walking up to the warehouse. Time to move.

When I rise to my feet, I draw the attention of one of the men by the dock.

"Hey! It's that Fuse guy!" he shouts.

Two of them run toward us while the other three rush to carry the rest of the boxes to the warehouse. They probably have a truck waiting inside.

Splitting up, Dean and I run in opposite directions. The man who spotted us pulls a small gun from his belt and shoots at us. I dive to the ground until the shots stop. When they do, I notice one of the guys from the warehouse is running right toward me with a rifle in his hands.

Not wanting to get too far from the dock, I spring to my feet and send a streak of lightning at my pursuer. He jumps back, his left hand letting go of his gun, which clatters to the ground beside him.

"Whoa!" he shouts.

Before he has a chance to pick the gun back up, I shoot lightning at it, flinging it out of his reach. He watches where it falls and then turns to me and raises his fists. I let the lightning crackle between my fingers, trying to intimidate him. We eye each other up without a word. He's probably trying to guess my next move, and I don't know what to say to keep that fear in him.

When he breaks into a run, I open my palm and hit him in the chest with a streak of lightning. He falls to the ground, clutching at his chest.

Running past him, I pick up the gun and toss it as far in the lake as I can before running to Dean. His attacker is lying still on the gravel near the dock entrance, flipped and disoriented. I've been there.

When I turn to make sure Dean's okay, he charges one of the

other two men carrying the final boxes from the boat.

I shoot another string of lightning at one of the men while I run, but I miss my target. Still, when Dean approaches, one of the men chases after him while another one follows me. For now, the boxes aren't going anywhere.

Sprinting toward the warehouse door, I stop as a bullet flies by my head. I spin on my heels and open my palm, zapping the man, leaving him convulsing on the ground.

I run to the two remaining boxes and try to carry one over to the water's edge, but a kick in my back drops me to the ground. I turn quickly, shooting lightning at the same time, but it doesn't connect with anything in particular. When my eyes find the kicker—the man who came in with the boat—he's standing stock-still, facing the street.

Finding Dean, I see he's looking up the driveway too. I follow his gaze and spot a large shadow moving in our direction.

Between my mask, the darkness, and the distance, it takes a minute for my eyes to focus on the figure, but he looks like he's limping. As he comes into the moonlight, I can't help but stare. His skin is drooping as if it's melting off his body. His face hangs so low that he looks like a bloodhound, although his skin shines in the moonlight like a bad burn scar.

The thugs open fire on him, and I still can't take my eyes off him as the bullets rip through his green jacket and seem to be *absorbed* into his skin. He makes no movement to indicate that they hurt him or even that he's bothered by them at all.

Dean is closest to him, and I get ready in case I need to zap. It's kind of a far distance to ensure accuracy, but it's the only move I have at the moment.

The man looks down lazily at Dean, but quickly looks back up at the thugs when they open fire again. As the shots ring out, Dean quickly rolls out of the way into the underbrush. He's not bleeding that I can tell, so that's good.

The second round of gunshots having done no better than the first, the thugs stop and watch as the newcomer takes them in. A moment later, he opens his mouth and roars, spewing brownish-orange fluid everywhere, splattering the men. I take a few steps back to make sure I'm out of range.

The men begin screaming horribly as the fluid fizzles on their skin. I try to keep my dinner down as their skin turns an angry red before it slowly drips off of their bodies.

I jump when Dean runs to my side and grabs my arm.

"Let's get the hell out of here," he says breathlessly.

I nod and look toward the fluid-spewer. He's staring right at us. Almost like we're his next victims. Before he has a chance to react, I put up my hands and zap him.

He turns away and moans. As he does, Dean and I sprint up the slope and back onto the busy city street, away from the freakish sight below.

———

"THAT WAS…WEIRD," Dean says when we get back to the apartment. He tosses his gloves on the counter and kneels down to untie his boots.

"Yeah. I wonder where that…thing is from. What happened to him to make him look like that?" I pull off my Fuse mask and gloves and lean back against the edge of the counter.

"I don't have an answer for you, man," he says, switching to the opposite foot. "But it makes you wonder how common mutation like that is."

"That's a question for Wes," I say.

"Way over my pay grade." He stands and walks to the corner where a stack of boxes from his apartment sits. He moves the top one over and riffles through the second one before pulling out a set of clothes. "I'm going to take a shower. Need to get in there?"

I shake my head, still too wrapped up in what happened by the lake. "No, I'm all set for now."

"Awesome. Thanks."

When the bathroom door closes, I step into my room to change out of my Fuse suit and into sweatpants and a T-shirt. After I grab a glass of water from the kitchen sink, I come back to the living room but trip over one of Dean's boxes on my way to the couch.

Chapter One

Ever since the police allowed him to clean out his apartment, he's had boxes stashed here. And now he's officially my roommate, on the lease and everything. But that also means that his stuff is laying all over the place.

When he moved in right before Christmas, we still hadn't talked about what happened that night with Alexander, so I didn't raise too many objections to him taking over my living room. But it's March now, so the clutter is way past the point of annoying.

"Why don't you turn on the TV?" Dean's voice breaks into my thoughts. I didn't even hear the bathroom door open.

"I don't know. I didn't think about it."

"Maybe the news will have something about what happened tonight." He carries his dirty clothes over to his duffel bag in the corner and stuffs it in with the rest of the clothes he wore this week.

I glance at the clock on my phone. "It's almost midnight. It wouldn't be on tonight."

"All right." He plops down in the chair to my right, on top of the pile of blankets he sleeps with.

"You know, you should probably get an actual hamper for your clothes so we don't have to smell that bag all week."

He looks down at his stuff and then up to me. "And put it where?"

I chuckle. "Does it matter? This place looks like it exploded since you moved in."

"Hey, I'm keeping everything as tidy as I can."

I shoot him a look.

"Okay, I'll clean up tomorrow. But I don't know how much better it'll be if I don't have any place to put this stuff."

He's right. The living room is the only space that's his. I'm sure he has to be crawling up the walls without his own domain.

I clear my throat. "This is a, uh, two-bedroom apartment, you know."

Dean looks unsure. "But what about—the couch is fine, Ethan. You don't have to do anything you're not ready for."

I shake my head. "No, it's fine. It's not like Cale's using his room right now anyway. I've just been…" I shrug. "What's the worst that can happen if you just use it for a little while?"

"Are you sure?"

Nodding, I say, "Yeah. I mean, Myra and I are holding out hope that Cale's still out there because we haven't seen proof of… anything." A body. I can't bring myself to even imagine Cale's corpse. "But it's fine."

"I know," Dean says. "You need closure, I get that. But if Cale's disappearance is what that Black Hand letter was warning…"

"There won't be a body to find," I finish for him. "I know. But at the same time, it's been four months since he disappeared, and you're probably getting tired of sleeping on the couch."

He shrugs. An admission.

I force a smile. "Well, I need you to get your crap out of the living room. I'm tired of looking at it."

Looking down, he smiles. "Yeah, yeah, yeah."

Glancing at my phone again, I see it's ten after twelve. "Well, I should get to bed."

"Yeah, me too. Now that I have an actual bed to go to."

I get up and walk around the couch. "If you mess anything up, I'm going to break your face."

He laughs. "I'd like to see you try."

"Oh, I will." I turn to head to my room.

"Hey. Thanks, Ethan."

Chapter Two

How long you been working for Tranidek?" JD asks as I drive through the lunch-hour traffic in one of the company's trucks. He's in a blue Wilkinson College sweatshirt with a reflective vest overtop of it. The company dress code is pretty lax when you're working in the field.

"Just since Thanksgiving," I reply. We inch up to the next stoplight, which turns red, and I groan. We're going to be late.

JD doesn't take notice. "You're from Wyatt too, right?"

He's the newest employee in our department, and Mr. Cowan wanted me to take him out in the field with me today to show him the ropes.

"Yup. I was IT tech support, which is quite different from what we're doing here."

"Gotcha. I was in development at Wyatt," he says. "I was kind of nervous about switching jobs because I thought I'd have to learn all new software."

I shake my head. "No, the software we've been developing is basically the same as what Wyatt's been using in their solar roadways. Actually, it's probably better because we can learn from some of their mistakes." I drive up one light farther. Only two more blocks and then I can turn onto Flint Parkway, where we needed to be five minutes ago.

"Oh cool." JD sits and watches the traffic for a minute before he breaks the silence again. "So explain to me again what we're doing today."

"Well, you know how Tranidek reached an agreement with Wyatt and the city to split the solar roadway project?"

He nods. "Yeah, that was back around the first of the year."

"Yup. Now that the solar panels are being installed, we just need to check to make sure they're all working properly." We were supposed to be there right after lunch, but I didn't think there'd be this much traffic in the middle of the day.

"But it's March. Why are they just installing them now?"

"Had to wait for the weather to break. Can't put the panels down on top of snow and ice."

We inch up to the next light, and I hit my signal to start to move into the turn lane.

"That makes sense," JD says. "And Tranidek got half of the city streets, right?"

"Well, sort of. The city limits were split in half, and since Wyatt had already started downtown, they get those streets and most of midtown."

"So the most mileage."

"But we get the rest, including the residential areas," I say. "There's even been talks of expanding into the suburbs once the panels in the city are fully installed."

"Really? That's good for the company."

I maneuver the truck to turn onto Flint.

"Yeah, their stocks have soared with the increased number of customers, so they're more willing to give out raises." My ninety-day review last week meant my paycheck got a noticeable bump. Along with Dean moving in, it's the reason I've been able to keep my apartment even with Cale gone.

"Well, hopefully I can cash into some of that wealth," JD says.

"I'm sure you will. If the company does well, that's better for everyone. And with a development background? You're probably doing pretty well for yourself already."

Now finally on Flint, I race down the tree-lined residential street that's already been covered in Tranidek's solar panels, then pull the truck behind the rest of the construction vehicles parked on the street.

"Come on," I tell JD as I grab my vest and tablet from the backseat. "We're late."

"Hey, Pierce! Come on, we're waiting," one of the crew members calls to me. He and several other men are sitting on the grass between the street and the sidewalk. "The other guy from Tranidek left ten minutes ago."

"Sorry! We got stuck in traffic." Hurrying over with my tablet, I kneel down and plug into the panel they just laid down and check the signal strength. The tablet beeps and turns green across the various diagnostics and signal measurements. This panel is just fine, like I'm sure most of them will be. I pull out the cord and give one of the workers a thumbs-up.

"It's good."

They move to the truck and grab another panel.

I step back to JD and explain to him how to test the panels and what to look for if something is off.

"It's important to test the strength of each panel, not only to ensure one hundred percent efficiency, but to make sure the city has a fully-functioning Grid," I explain. "If even one panel is out, it weakens the Grid across the whole city."

"Sounds tedious."

"It is, but since we're moving at such a rapid pace, it's a good idea to double-check our work."

"This is going to take awhile to get everything laid out," JD says.

I watch as the workers lay another heavy panel down and start to hook it up with the existing ones. "Well, not exactly. The success of the company lately has expedited the project, and Rizzoli and the board want us to get as much done as we can before the fall, when the weather turns again."

"Do you think that's doable?"

I rock my head back and forth, thinking. "Flint Parkway is one of the first streets to have Tranidek-installed solar panels, but at the rate we're moving—even though it's tedious—we probably could cover our parts of the city in the timeframe Rizzoli wants. That's the hope, at least."

I have JD check the next solar panel, watching over his shoulder and walking him through each step. I ignore the complaints coming from the workers. I don't blame them for being annoyed, but I'm just doing my job.

We plop on the strip of grass between the street and sidewalk as we wait for the workers to install the next panel and I get started on my hourly progress report to send back to Mr. Cowan at the office.

I volunteered to work in the field for a couple days to get out of the office, but I wish I had time at a computer to really look into that saggy skin guy from last night. I still can't get the image out of my head of his spit literally making the skin of those crooks melt and sizzle. Just when I thought I'd seen it all, something else pops up to give me nightmares.

I texted Wes this morning to see if he's come across any other mutation cases, but he said he hasn't seen any. Even though he's still teaching a few courses at Olympia University, he spends most of his working hours at the clinic with Alex. So his work is less focused on mutations nowadays and more on people with a bad cough.

As I walk back over to test the next panel the workers just laid, I try to rationalize where the man-creature came from. He and I are similar because we're both mutants of some sort, but while I just got a nasty scar and a perpetual electric charge running through my body, his transformation was so drastic that it affected not only his ability to spit acid but also his appearance. Let's just say I'm glad to have the mutant card I was dealt.

We continue to work our way north along Flint Parkway from Main Street to Ashland Avenue, me and JD taking turns checking the panels. Around two o'clock we reach Winchester Avenue. I know this area better now that I've been here on more than one occasion. This part of the city, notably along the parkways, is filled with wealthy residents. The rows of brownstone townhouses are occasionally broken up by large mansions with big yards and perfectly manicured gardens. It's all centered around the Olympia Country Club, which many of these residents belong to.

The quiet streets and the skyline views are what attracted people to the area when it was first developed. Granted, when they ran I-123 right through the neighborhood in the fifties, that forced some residents out, but for the most part, this area is still very high profile.

Among the people who live out here are Mayor Eugene Banks, Olympia businessman Edward Fordham, and, oh yeah, Carlo Martelli. With only a few credible sources of income, the Martellis have managed to worm their way into the lifestyles of some of the most elite residents in the city. Surprise, surprise.

I'm momentarily pulled out of my head when the next panel I scan flashes red on my tablet. The word "Faulty" is displayed across the screen.

"So what's that mean?" JD asks beside me.

"It's no good," I say with a sigh. I get up and find Hank Mc-Curdy, the project manager.

"All done, then? Can we move on?" He's annoyed Tranidek sent me out here to check his work. Feels like he's being babysat and that I'm only slowing things down. But warnings like the one I just got are the reason I'm here.

"You gotta take that last one out." I show him my screen.

He raises his eyebrows slightly. "We're supposed to finish this stretch in another hour. If we take one out, we'll be in the way once rush hour hits."

"What good's it doing if it doesn't even work?" I snap. "I'm just doing my job."

"Fine," he grumbles as he walks back to his crew.

I watch as they remove it, swapping it out with another panel. I explain to JD again why it's important that the panels are all checked. If this one had been left, it would've messed everything up for us back at the office.

Stepping forward, I'm about to plug into the new panel when

I hear a man screaming. I look around at the workers, thinking one of them must've been the one to shout, but the scream sounds more agonizing than that. And farther away.

Setting my tablet on the ground, I take off in a sprint toward the source of the noise. It's farther away than I thought, but as I round the corner onto Winchester Avenue, the sound of the man's voice grows even louder, and I can see him writhing on the ground in front of one of the houses toward the end of the street.

Martelli's street.

I stop short when I approach him. His hands are covering his face—or rather, what's left of it. Like the men from last night, his skin is melting and sizzling as it slides off his body, dripping onto the grass in a gooey pile.

Turning away to keep from vomiting, I look around for the man-creature, but I don't see him. Instead, my eyes land on Martelli's house. The gate at the end of his driveway is closed tight.

Most of the people living on Winchester are related to the Martellis. This man rolling on the ground is probably one of them.

Two of the workers catch up to me. One says, "Oh my God, oh my God, oh my God" over and over again. The other turns away and takes a deep breath before pulling out his phone and calling 9-1-1.

"Are you okay?" he asks me when he gets off the phone.

I nod, still unable to keep my eyes off the man writhing on the ground. I need to find this mutant.

———

THE SCENT OF garlic hits me when I walk in the door after work. Dean's back is to me as he stirs something on the stove. He looks over his shoulder and says, "Hey, it's almost ready."

"Okay, just give me a minute." I disappear in the bathroom.

On my way out, I stop into Cale's old room to see what Dean's done with it. Other than the boxes stacked in the corner, everything looks the same, which isn't saying much. Cale was a slob. From the stacks of papers on top of his dresser to the dust collecting on every flat surface, it looks almost as bad as he left it. If anything, Dean may have had to pick up the room a little bit to use it.

When I return to the kitchen, two bowls of pasta sit on the counter near the barstools.

Dean sets the pot in the sink and takes a seat at the counter.

"How was working in the field today?" He pokes at his dinner, blowing on it to cool it.

I take my seat. "Not bad…until I saw someone else's face get melted off."

He lets out a breath of air and rubs his neck as if it's stiff. "Of course there was another one."

I nod. "Yep. No sign of the guy from last night, though. Well, other than the whole face-dripping-off thing. From what I gathered when the police questioned me today, they don't know anything either."

"Who was the victim? Where'd you see it?"

"Well, that's the thing. He was on, uh, Winchester Avenue."

"He was? Was my father there? Joe? Rizzo? Did anyone else see?"

I shake my head. "No. Nobody was around. It was actually kind of…weird."

"Well, they have jobs, Ethan. Even if they are illegal. My father goes across town all the time to meet with someone or another."

"And he takes his guards with him?"

Dean shrugs. "Usually, yeah."

"I just think it's awful coincidental that the attack happened on that street when no one was around. Especially the way he was attacked. It's disturbing."

Dean grins. "You're Fuse. You should be used to disturbing by now."

"Pardon me for not being desensitized to the world yet."

He holds up his free hand. "Only a matter of time."

"I've been thinking about this guy, and he's just weird. Not natural at all. Did he escape from a lab or something? Was he electrocuted like me? Where did this guy come from?"

"Well, I doubt he was electrocuted," Dean says before taking another bite of his food.

"Why not? I mutated when I was electrocuted."

"You developed an ability to *shoot lightning*. Why would this guy turn into Quasimodo from a lightning strike and not just develop powers like you?"

I shrug. "I don't know."

"Did you talk to Alex or Wes about it?"

"Yeah, I texted Wes, but he hasn't seen anything."

"Gotcha."

I stab my fork into my food. "Anyway, how was your day? I see you moved your boxes out." The living room looks tidy, almost empty.

He looks over at where his stuff used to be. "I told you I would. I even vacuumed."

"How long have you been home?"

"My last appointment canceled, and I was able to bump my shrink appointment up, so I got home early."

I nod and take another bite. Dean's been seeing a therapist about everything that happened with James Alexander, both when he was a kid and just a few months ago. He doesn't like to admit it, but I can tell it's helping. He doesn't seem as down all the time anymore, and he's more willing to talk about that night, even though I still try to avoid the subject.

"Did you look into this man-creature at all?" I ask. "Or the gun shipment?"

Still chewing, Dean gets up to grab something from the coffee table in the living room. He comes back and drops today's newspaper in front of me. There's a dark picture of a group of policemen at the dock from last night with police tape in the foreground. The headline reads, "*Three die in firearm smuggle attempt.*"

Three bodies were found last night along the shores of Olympia Lake almost completely skinless. The victims showed signs of being burned alive. Residents report witnessing a 'monster' fleeing the scene.

The picture caption reads, "*Three men died at the hands of an alleged 'monster' witnesses named 'Fizz.'*"

"Fizz?" I ask. I suppose that's an accurate enough description of the attacks.

"I know. Kind of weird. Fuse and Fizz."

"I wonder if any of the witnesses saw us." Surprisingly, there's no mention of Fuse anywhere in the article.

Dean shakes his head. "I don't think so. Flip to page ten."

I open it up and scan the page until I notice the headline at the top of the opinion section. "*Councilwoman Connors doesn't follow through.*" My eyes skim through the article, which blames Myra for the increased gang violence in Hopman, citing several incidents that I've taken care of as Fuse, but saying last night's attack was the last straw.

After winning the special election in December and becoming the newest member of city council, Miss Myra Connors has stated that her intent is to breathe life back into the Hopman neighborhood, suggesting far-fetched ideas that require tax dollars and nonexistent community involvement. With the recent bizarre and deadly attacks in the neighborhood since Connors took over for former councilman Frank Lloyd, perhaps Olympians—particularly those living in Hopman—have traded one devil for another.

"This is ridiculous!" I say when I finish reading. "She's been on the council for only four months! She's still cleaning up messes left over from Frank Lloyd. How can they expect her to have all the answers already?"

Dean shrugs. "I don't know. But it's only an opinion piece. I thought it was over-the-top, myself, but that's the way the world works. Actually, that's the way this city works."

"Who even wrote this? It doesn't say."

"Looks like they *forgot* to include a byline. My guess is it was someone else at city hall. Someone who doesn't like the way Myra called out Frank Lloyd for his involvement with my father."

Fuse: Oblivion

I should've known this would happen. Should've known that even after Myra got in office that she wouldn't have an easy road ahead of her. Hopefully she's not blindsided by this attack like I am. I just hope it's not weighing her down too much with everything else on her plate—especially Cale.

Chapter Three

Myra answers the door with a steaming bowl of soup in her hand cradled by a paisley potholder. She looks like the epitome of exhaustion: she has bags under her eyes and a lazy braid on her shoulder and is wearing gray sweatpants and one of Cale's Olympia University hoodies.

When she sees me, she pulls at the strings of the hoodie with her free hand as if to hide her appearance. "Oh, I didn't know you were coming…"

"Sorry. Can I come in?"

She moves aside and closes the door behind me after I step in. Her apartment is in a converted old warehouse, so it's very spacious. Industrial modern, I think they call it. The exposed metallic air vents run along the ceiling near the exposed brick outer wall. Hardwood floors lead right to the spare bedroom, the doorway of which sits under the staircase to the master loft.

No doubt about it, this girl makes good money. Too bad it's been coming at the expense of her credibility lately.

"Come to check up on me?" She leans on the granite countertop, using her spoon to play with the chunks in her soup.

I take a seat at the counter. "Well, yeah. I haven't seen you in a few weeks."

"Yeah. Sorry about that. I've been busy with work and haven't really been up for guests."

Since Cale disappeared, we've been getting together every week or so to check in with each other. But between her demanding job at city hall and mine as Fuse, we've been neglecting our dinner dates. Still, it doesn't mean we don't need to lean on each other anymore. Cale and Myra dated for almost four years. He was going to propose. To me, she's basically family.

I nod. "I get it."

"Yeah." Her eyes remain on her meal, although she doesn't make an effort to eat any of it.

"Have you seen the paper lately?"

Finally, she looks up at me. "If you mean the *Tribune*, then no. I haven't looked at it since I've basically become Satan to them."

I let out a halfhearted chuckle to try to alleviate the tension, but it doesn't work. Her attention shifts back down to her soup, her spoon clinking against the bowl.

"I think it's unfair what they're doing to you," I finally say after another few seconds of silence passes.

"Yeah, well, you're about the only one." Her eyes flicker to me for a moment with a hint of curiosity. "What are they saying about me this time?"

"That you're the reason violent crime in Hopman is increasing." I look up at her and quickly add, "It's ridiculous."

She rolls her eyes. "They're a bunch of fucking liars."

I jolt because Myra usually never swears.

"One of the first things I did when I was elected was get in touch with the OPD about the violence in my district," she continues. "Violent crimes have been increasing across the *entire city*, not just Hopman."

That stings.

"Isn't Fuse helping to drop that rate?" I ask.

"Sort of. Overall, crime is down across the city, but the proportion of violent crimes is growing."

Chapter Three

"So the crimes that are committed are more along the lines of murder and assault than petty thefts."

"Exactly."

I wonder if my vigilantism has sparked others to take matters into their own hands or if the actions of the Martellis are more to blame for this spike in violence.

"And what kind of sources is the *Tribune* using?" Myra goes on. "What happened to maintaining *their* credibility as a trustworthy news source? As long as they have someone to blame, it doesn't matter, apparently."

"I know. It's not fair. I'm sorry this is happening to you. But do you think that their reaction to you doing your job is just proof that you're doing something right? I'd be disappointed if you just kept things status quo from Frank Lloyd's time in office."

She sighs. "That'd be easier to accept if my constituents weren't afraid to live where they do. If it wasn't the bad egg among the other city districts."

"Myra, you're still new to this job," I remind her. "You'll figure it out. You just have to find your stride."

"Yeah." She comes over and takes the seat next to me at the breakfast bar. Setting her bowl down, she wraps her arm around mine and leans on my shoulder. "I miss Cale."

"Me too."

"He always knew what to say when I was discouraged."

I feel a twinge of guilt because I *don't* know what to say to motivate her. So instead I don't say anything and just let her talk.

"He used to tell me that I was going to be president someday, and that eventually I'd look back at my issues in Olympia and smile." Her voice goes hollow. "Not much to smile about nowadays."

I rest my head against hers. "Well...I'm not sure I see you as president, only because I'd miss you too much here, but I will say this: you'll get through this. Everything happens for a reason."

"You really think so?"

"Of course."

"Then why was Cale taken from me? From us?"

I let out a sigh and am reminded of both Cale and Emma. It

doesn't seem fair that they're gone. "I don't know."

"I miss him so much."

"Yeah," I say softly.

She sits up. "Not only because of him—I mean, obviously I do miss him. That's probably why I've been working so much lately. But I also miss him as a reporter. He always made sure to be as honest as he could be."

I grin. "That's true. He always had the scoop on everything and was full of so much trivia. He knew this city inside and out."

"He was thorough, yeah. Probably why his story on the Works never saw the light of day."

I'm not sure what Myra knows about Cale's involvement with Leon Wallace, who is the developer of the Works and also one of Martelli's made men. I've tried to investigate Wallace, but without concrete evidence against him, my hands are tied. I thought I could go after him as Fuse, but Dean pointed out that now that Carlo knows my identity, it could result in someone else getting hurt. Maybe even Myra. It was Cale's investigation into Wallace that got him in trouble with Martelli.

"Anyway," she says. "I don't know why we're talking about him like he's dead. Nothing's ruled out until we know something for sure, right?"

I pause and study my hands. Are we just kidding ourselves believing that Cale could be alive somewhere? It's very likely that the Martelli family are behind his disappearance. That means he's probably dead and we need to start moving on.

"Right, Ethan?" she pushes.

I give a tight smile and nod. "Right."

"It's a shame, though," she continues without a comment on my pause. "They're breaking ground on that complex next week."

I let out a heavy sigh. "I know." Just like that, the story that was going to be Cale's big break is gone. Worse, the project will put a large number of families at risk. "But you did what you could to stop it."

"Yeah."

This whole media fire Myra's been under started when she began to vote against the redevelopment of the Works at city council meetings. It only intensified when she tried to dig up evidence to show that it was a bad deal.

"Well, thanks to the *Tribune* and some of my fellow council-members doubting my abilities to do my job, I need to go to the stupid ribbon cutting for good press." She carries her soup bowl to the sink and rinses it out.

"That sucks."

"Yeah. Hopefully nobody will ask me to make a statement about the project." She picks up the dish towel to dry her hands and leans back against the counter. "But if I say anything about the environmental review, I know my words will be twisted to sound like I'm against *any* development in Olympia. Or poor people," she adds with an eye roll.

"I guess the only thing you can do is prove them wrong by doing the work that'll move Hopman and the whole city forward."

"Easier said than done, but I do have a few ideas. Problem is, some of the power players aren't taking me seriously because I had no competition when I ran for council. There was James Alexander for a bit, but he didn't even end up on the ballot."

"Well, you're in now. So get to work." I stretch in my seat before getting up and moving to the door.

She smirks. "Yeah, I know. I'm just being a downer because of Cale. It's been a rough day and I could've used him. But you helped."

I smile. "Well, just keep me in mind. If you ever need to talk or anything—"

"I know. Thanks for coming tonight. I needed to see a friendly face."

I give her a hug. "Anytime."

———

WHEN I GET home, Dean is facing the window in the living room talking on the phone.

"…be careful." He turns and smiles to me quickly before looking out the window again. I fill a glass of water at the sink and try not to eavesdrop. In such a small apartment, though, there aren't a lot of places I can go.

"No, I don't live there anymore," he continues. "I've actually moved in with Ethan."

My ears perk up.

"He's good. Really likes his job, but you probably already knew that."

I lean against the counter and sip my water.

"Listen, I need to go.... Yeah, maybe next week. Talk to you soon.... You too. Bye." He clicks off and slides his phone in his back pocket as he turns around. "How's Myra?"

I take a seat on the couch, anxious to ask him who he was talking to, but decide not to pry.

"She's hanging in there. Misses Cale, stressed about her job and the negative attention from the media."

He takes a seat on the other end of the couch. "I can imagine. But...she's okay? Like, really okay?"

I shrug. "I guess. As well as she can be, you know?"

"Yeah." He picks away some of the fuzz from the couch cushion. "What about you? How are you holding up?"

"Actually, not bad." I offer a grin to try to convince him but he doesn't buy it.

"Ethan..."

"Don't get me wrong. I miss him. I hate it that he's...gone or whatever, but...I don't know." I lean my head back against the cushion and talk to the ceiling. "I think after what I went through with Emma and almost losing yo—" I stop myself before venturing into the off-limits territory of me and Dean. "After Emma, I think I'm doing better at handling these types of things."

He shakes his head. "It's not supposed to get easier to handle people close to you dying—"

"He's not dead," I cut in. "Not until we see a body." Even though I know it's foolish, I can't help but think that saying it over and over will make it true. Voicing my doubts that he's alive would feel like I'm laying him to rest. Like it was his time to die. I can't accept that.

Dean lets out a breath of air. "Either way, losing someone

like that—even if it is temporary—is always hard. Part of what makes us human."

This conversation is getting too uncomfortable. Too intimate. I can't let myself get closer to Dean. If he's not ready to be with anyone, I'd be getting my hopes up for nothing. I can't take any other negativities in my life right now. I need to deflect.

I smirk. "But I'm not human. I've…mutated."

Dean rolls his eyes and shakes his head. "That was such a bad joke."

"Admit it, it was funny."

"Not really."

"Come on, you're trying not to laugh."

He grins. "Fine! Okay, I'm laughing, but just because you're such an idiot."

I chuckle, feeling very proud of myself.

"But really," he continues, "are you sure you're doing okay? We haven't really talked about it much, and then last night when you gave me his room it seemed like you'd accepted things—"

"I was just tired of you sleeping on the couch."

He turns away from me. "Okay." After a few seconds of silence, he says, "Speaking of mutants, what are we going to do about this Fizz guy?"

I let out a deep breath. "I don't really know yet. This is the first I've heard of him, but maybe he's been around without us realizing it."

"What do you mean by that?"

"Well, he had to come from somewhere. Had to have time to turn into what he is now. I mean, look at me. I was in a coma for a while before I woke up, and I don't look anything like him."

"Well…" Dean smirks.

I swat at him. "I'll see if I can dig around online for anything that might indicate how he got to be this way."

"And then what?"

I shrug. "I don't know. But if he's killing people, then he needs to be stopped."

"Right."

"Who were you talking to on the phone?" If he can talk to

me about Cale, I think I can push into his business a little bit.

"My, uh, father."

My eyes grow wide and I shift on the couch to face him. After Carlo uninvited Dean to Christmas two days before—claiming that the family didn't react well to him being at Thanksgiving—we agreed he would cut all personal ties to him. To my knowledge, Dean hasn't talked to Carlo since.

"What did he want?" I ask.

"Well, that man you saw the other day near Flint—the one whose face was melting?"

"Yeah, what about him?"

"He was my father's cousin Luca."

I narrow my eyes but quickly correct them, trying to hide any sign of judgment from my face.

"Were you guys close?" I ask.

Dean shakes his head. "No, but my father was. You met Luca at Thanksgiving, remember?"

"No, I met so many people that day. And he looked a little different the last time I saw him. Are you going to his funeral?"

"After the last get-together and not being invited to Christmas, I think it's pretty obvious that I don't fit in with my family anymore."

"So your dad just called to tell you Luca was dead?"

"Yeah, I guess," Dean responds.

"Why?"

He looks at me, surprised. "He's still family, Ethan."

I drop my eyes. "You're right, I'm sorry. My point was—"

"My father thinks Luca's death was meant as a message from Michael Bello. He thinks Bello's got a full team and wants to be the only mobster in town."

"By melting off someone's face? Haven't you guys ever sent a text or picked up the phone?"

"Funny."

"How is Bello even supposed to build a team? Isn't he still in witness protection?"

Dean nods. "As far as I know. He's probably in touch with someone back here who's putting together a team for him."

"How is he managing that under police surveillance?"

He shrugs. "I don't know."

"Okay," I say with a hint of disbelief. "So what message was Bello sending with Luca's death?"

"Well, my father thinks the acid is a sign. He thinks Luca's murderer got it from the Works and that it'll throw the police off their trail. My father's contacts have strong influences at the Works. They're breaking ground next week."

"Your father's a little anxious, isn't he?" I ask.

"Well, the police still haven't moved in on anyone after the dirt Bello gave them, so he's a little on edge. Thinks it'll be any day now that something bad will happen, and he doesn't feel prepared for it. And it's not like he can face Bello himself since he's in witness protection. He's fighting an invisible enemy, and that makes him nervous."

"Which makes him paranoid."

"Exactly."

"But isn't it more likely that it's Fizz and *not* Bello? Which is why we need to figure out the mutant's M.O."

"We know that because we saw Fizz," Dean counters. "My father didn't."

"So what's he going to do?"

He shrugs. "I don't know, exactly. But if I know my father, he's going to do something."

"Like what? Kill the people on Bello's team?"

"Maybe."

"I thought you said he's not a killer?"

"The circumstances have changed, Ethan! My father didn't kill Bello for betraying him, and now he's faced with those consequences. Not acting would make it seem like attacking my father and his men goes without consequence."

I let out a deep breath and shift gears. "What did you say when he told you about Luca?"

"Just thanked him for letting me know."

"That's it?"

"What did you want me to say?"

I shrug. "I don't know."

"He'll probably want to get a sense of what kind of man-power Bello has—if it's even him behind it."

"I thought we agreed to distance ourselves from your father? Seems like you can't draw that line."

"He was calling to warn me, Ethan. Like it or not, I'm a Martelli by blood. Just because my father says I'm out of the business doesn't mean I'm off limits to everyone."

I bite my bottom lip to keep my words in. Anything that comes out now will certainly be followed by regret later. We sit in silence, both of us refusing to talk. The fact that Dean even took a call from his father scares me. How easily will he be pulled back into the family?

After we've calmed down a few minutes later, I say in a forced calm voice, "After things like this, I wonder if I can trust you like I think I can. I know you've had my back in the past, but what if a day comes where you don't?"

Another uncomfortable admission, but I'd rather feel awkward than angry. We've tried anger before, and it doesn't work. Talking things out will, at the very least, get my point across.

Dean's voice softens. "Ethan, you basically heard our whole conversation. Other than Luca and suggesting that there will be consequence for his death, my father didn't mention anything else about the business. Hell, he even asked how you were doing."

I tighten my lips to try to hide my smile, but based on Dean's reaction, he sees it anyway.

"You have nothing to worry about with me," he continues. "For better or worse, you know everything about me. If I thought for a second my father was trying to recruit me again, you'd be the first person I'd tell."

Finally, I meet his eyes and smile. "Good."

Even though the last few months have shown it, it's nice to hear Dean confirm that he's definitely on my side. Still, I would be happier if I didn't have to deal with the threat of his father anymore.

Chapter Four

This is stupid," Dean mutters to me as we jog down deserted Jefferson Street. It's almost three in the morning, but I wanted to be absolutely sure that nobody would see us. Especially Dean, who refuses to wear a disguise other than a hoodie.

"Just keep an eye out," I respond, peering around the corner of a building to check if the coast is clear before waving Dean on.

It was my idea to check out Luca Martelli's body at the city morgue. There has to be some sort of chemical residue on the body. If we can figure out what it is, maybe we can determine where it came from to get a better idea of who did this.

Then again, the most obvious suspect is Fizz, but I don't know what the hell I'm looking for on Luca's body if it is. Did Fizz shoot those guys by the lake with acid or some unknown substance? Does the spray from Fizz even contain natural elements?

Peering around the next corner, I check to see if there are any security guards around. The morgue is right behind the federal courthouse near the city's police headquarters and jail.

Fuse: Oblivion

The First Olympian Medical Center is on the other side of the morgue, across West Division Street.

With all of these important buildings so close to one another, it's no surprise that this place is under constant surveillance. I already hacked into the cameras through the Grid to put up a decoy scene for a specific half-hour block, but we need to be in and out by then and *not* run into any guards. No wonder Dean said this plan was stupid.

On the next street over, I take a quick inventory of the folks who might be a problem for us. There's one guard patrolling the back entrance of the courthouse, but he doesn't seem to be on high alert. The real problem is the number of police officers coming in and out of the station adjacent to the morgue. Even where we're standing feels exposed.

"What about the loading dock?" Dean whispers behind me, making me jump. "It's over on the hospital side."

"On West Division?" That's a busy street. Even at this hour.

"It's our best option."

True. "What about cameras? I didn't think we'd come in that way, so I didn't check those cameras."

"I doubt they're being monitored regularly, anyway. You'll just have to zap whatever ones you see and try not to be spotted by them in the process."

Seems too easy. Still, I can't think of a better way. And I'm not a fan of breaking security devices that are meant to prevent break-ins…like the one we're doing now. But the clock is ticking.

"Fine, but stay here," I tell him.

Sprinting across the street toward the morgue, I keep close to the building as I run alongside it. When I get to the loading dock bay, I spot two cameras on each side of the two overhead loading doors. Holding out my hand, I summon the energy flowing in me and pray to God that I'll stay out of view of the cameras.

One quick zap to each and they're out. Glass cracked, they both turn down. I look back and wave Dean forward.

After we each pull ourselves up on the loading dock, we notice the door is locked with a passcode. Holding my palm over the keypad, I prepare to shock it, but Dean grabs my arm.

Chapter Four

"What happened to leaving it the way we left it?" he asks.

"Then how do you suggest we get in?"

He looks around and then points to the vent grate near the pavement.

I groan. "You won't wear a suit but you'll crawl through a dusty air vent in a building for dead people?"

He ignores me and crouches down to yank at the grate. "It's not budging. You'll have to zap it."

"That'll break it."

"Just zap the fucking thing so we can get out of here!"

"Fine." Placing my palms over the top two screws, I let electricity trickle through me until the metal is weak enough for us to break the grate away from the wall.

"After you," he says.

Sighing, I kneel down to the vent. It's small but still big enough for us to squeeze in. Even Dean. As I crouch down to eye level with it, I'm hit by the stench of death. Nothing rotting—not like Dean's apartment when Alexander was using it as his personal torture chamber—but more like sterilized bad meat.

Remembering the time crunch, I press on. As I move deeper into the duct, the darkness grows. I have to rely on my hands to feel my way.

"Probably so many things living in here," I mutter.

"Quit whining and go!"

I follow the length of the tunnel, hoping that there aren't any security guards patrolling the halls. The decoy stills I put on the camera feeds won't do us any good if we come face-to-face with a security guard.

After a few minutes, I come to the first offshoot to a hallway. Soft light bleeds into the air vent and illuminates it.

"This way?" I ask behind me.

"Yeah, I'm getting a little claustrophobic in here."

"This was your idea."

"Uh, no, I believe this little rendezvous was *your* idea."

I ignore him.

The vent continues past the grate leading to the hall, and I use the extra room to swing my legs around. I shift on my back and press my feet against the grate. I kick at it until it gives way and crashes to the floor with a loud clatter.

I swear under my breath and listen for any movement coming from down the hall.

Nothing.

Turning around, I peek my head out and look into the hallway. The opening is near the ceiling, but the drop down isn't far. Every other light in the hallway is off, and judging by the lack of attention to the noise, nobody is patrolling.

Slinking out of the air duct, I wait for Dean to join me before we move forward.

"Any idea where Luca's body is?"

"This way." Dean takes off at a jog down the hallway, leading me around the corner and stopping to look for only a moment before turning into a cold room. The back wall is filled with large filing-cabinet type drawers—likely holding the bodies. A metal examination table sits in the middle, with a large light overhead. In the corner, separated by a curtain, a desk sits with papers stacked in various piles.

It smells worse in here. Still nothing rotten, but there's no hiding the fact that we're in the presence of corpses. Add that to the heightened clinical smell, and it's a wonder people actually work in here day in and day out.

"How did you know where to go?" I ask.

"While you were doing your thing with the cameras, I was pulling up the morgue blueprints."

"Oh."

"Besides," he says, approaching the desk, "I've been here before. A long time ago."

Right. Back in his mafia days.

We sift through the stack of reports on the desk until I find the one that reads "Luca Martelli."

"What's it say?" Dean asks as I flip through it.

"He died from severe burns," I reply.

"Only technically." He leaves my side to start pulling open drawers of bodies while I continue to read. As he opens each drawer, the dead smell gets worse. Luckily I'm wearing a mask to hide it a little bit.

Forcing myself to continue, I read the rest of the report, including the description of the condition of the body, some photos of it, even a toxicology report. All of it points to severe burns, which would explain why that was listed as the cause of death. None of it seems to really—

Wait. There's a list of substances found on the victim.

"Ethan, come look at this," Dean calls to me before I can tell him what I've found.

I step over to the body Dean has pulled out and am immediately met with the faceless Luca Martelli. I have to turn away at the sight of his exposed skull. Seeing pictures is one thing, but this is something else entirely.

"Look at where the acid melted or burned his skin." He grabs a pen from the desk and points to the edge of the burn marks. The skin looks like melted plastic right next to the bone.

Scanning the rest of his body, I notice that his face seems to be the only thing that was affected, other than his hands. And I know that's only because he grabbed his face when he got hit.

"If someone did throw acid at this guy, it would be more of a splatter, right?" Dean pushes.

I shrug. "I guess so. I don't really know."

"Well, think of a glass of water. If I threw it in your face, that wouldn't be the only thing that got wet, right?" He moves the pen to hover over Luca's neck and chest. "And there aren't even really any drip marks."

"Depends on how close he was standing."

"True, but whoever did this would've had to sneak up on him," Dean says. "If Luca fought them off at all, there would be splatter."

"Unless it was that Fizz guy. Maybe Luca didn't notice him until he opened the door."

"Maybe. What does the report say about what type of acid this was?"

"Oh yeah, I was going to show you that." I flip through until I find it again. "Um…possible chemicals include sulfuric acid, hydrochloric acid, sodium hydroxide, lime, and silver nitrate. It's quite the list."

"And if my college chemistry is coming back to me, none of those alone would actually *melt* someone's skin. They'd just be really bad burns."

"You think it's a mix of all of them?" I ask.

"Probably, yeah."

"Where would somebody get all of that and why would they mix them? Wouldn't that be too risky for the attacker? One drip could burn *their* skin off."

"Well, like you said, it's gotta be the Fizz guy." Dean looks down at Luca again.

"Okay, so it's Fizz. But Carlo thinks it was Bello." Meaning he's planning a retaliation for nothing. Violent attacks are already on the rise in this city. That rate will only continue to climb if—

The sound of an alarm makes me jump, but it silences when Dean pulls out his phone.

"Downloaded a police scanner app," he says with a smirk. "It alerts me whenever there's something big going on."

I cover Luca back up to get him out of my sight. "What's going on?"

"Shootout in Hopman. Adams Street, near Broad and Powers. Want to check it out?"

Sliding the drawer back in place, I say, "Might as well. It's not like I'm going to sleep anytime soon. Let's get the hell out of here."

Tossing the report back on the coroner's desk, we head to the vent and crawl our way back out to the street. Luckily, the decoy stills seem to be working. Outside, we run to where Dean's bike is parked off of Lake Street and head down West Division Street to Hopman.

As we get closer to Broad and Powers, the sound of gunshots erupts from the scene. With his helmet on, Dean is able to zip by without being detected.

There are two groups of men shooting at each other from either side of the street, hiding behind parked cars. It's too dangerous. We need to find another way to get in there without getting shot ourselves. I point Dean down an alley around the back of the buildings.

"What are you doing?" he asks when he comes to a stop.

"Going to see if I can get the upper hand from the roof." I reach for the bottom rung of the fire escape ladder.

"Need backup?"

"I need you more as a getaway. Keep an eye out and don't get shot."

At the top, I rush to the front of the building, ducking down low to stay out of sight. Peeking my head over, I locate six men on the opposite side of the street. Three are shooting, one is re-loading from the back seat of the car, and another is bleeding, with the final guy tending to him. They're all dressed in pea coats and business suits. A strange choice in outfits for a shootout. Reminds me of what Martelli's men would wear.

I stand a little taller and peer over. Everyone is too preoc-cupied with the shootout to notice me. I count five guys on my side of the street. They're dressed in hoodies and flannel jackets, similar to the guys at the territorial shootout I broke up a few months ago on Adams Street. Only two of the men on this side are shooting, while a third tends to the two other men who are bleeding out on the sidewalk.

As I weigh my options, I hear the faint sound of police sirens in the distance. I just need to buy time until they get here. And make sure none of the cops get hurt when they take these thugs into custody.

I hold my palm out toward the pavement in the street and strike the ground with a sharp bolt of lightning. The shooting ceases, but I've given away my location. One of the well-dressed men shifts his gun up to me. I duck away before he fires and race down the fire escape to Dean.

Back in the alley, blue lights flash as police cars whiz by to barricade the street. We need to get out of here. Even if the shooters don't chase us, it doesn't mean the police won't.

I'm barely on the back of the bike before Dean speeds out of the alley, narrowly missing a police car as we turn onto Broad

Street. The bike jerks to the right and I squeeze Dean tighter to hold on. I turn to see who, if anyone, is chasing us. A line of policemen is blocking the street where the shootout was, hidden behind their car doors and pointing their guns toward the action.

As we ride farther away, I spot the same green jacket that Fizz wore the other night along one of the side streets.

Smacking Dean's shoulder, I shout, "You have to turn around and follow him!"

"Who?"

"Just trust me!"

Dean makes a wide turn and goes back in the direction we came. The policemen are no longer hidden behind their cars now. They must be approaching the shooters and will have everything under control soon. That's good, but right now we need to follow Fizz.

I point Dean down the street where I saw Fizz, but there's no sign of him. He's on foot, so he can't have gone too far. We zigzag down a couple more streets looking for him. Amid the cracked sidewalks, broken windows, and parked cars, we don't see him anywhere.

Dean stops several blocks from the shootout, at the corner of Thomas Street and Whitney Place. We got farther away from the scene than I expected.

"I think we lost him," he says.

"Yeah," I mutter, disappointed.

"Sounds like the shooting stopped too. Do you want to just go home?"

It's probably going on four in the morning. Even though tomorrow—well today, technically—is Saturday, I know it'll be a rough one. I'm exhausted and discouraged but still have a lot of work to do to find Fizz and figure out why he killed Luca. Or those men by the water.

But first, I need sleep.

"Yeah, let's go."

Cutting down the other end of Powers Street to Wilkinson Avenue, we make our way back to the apartment.

Chapter Five

To me, the epitome of a waste of time is a ground-breaking ceremony. I don't need to see a bunch of suits sport hard-hats and move a little dirt for a photo shoot to show that a project is getting started. Despite the egos of the men and women in the top floors of corporate America, nobody cares that they were a part of the development. But money talks, and with the Works, it seems to shout.

Everyone is dressed to the nines, as am I. It's a funny sight because the Works is such a dump right now. We're all huddled under a large tent with the back half open so the complex can be seen behind the podium. There are a couple heaters, but the damp breeze still carries through.

"It really is a special day for Olympia," I overhear Leon Wallace tell one of the reporters. As the developer for the project, he's surrounded by reporters. "The fact that we can take this large, unused property and put it back on the tax rolls while providing homes for low-income families is really what this city is all about."

I roll my eyes and turn away. I guess I'm just cranky because

I don't want to be at this stupid ceremony. Not when Cale was doing everything he could to expose it for the scam that it is. This development feels like a step backward for the city.

I pull out my phone to see if Myra's texted me. I haven't spotted her yet, and I wonder if she changed her mind about coming.

"Put that away, you're representing the company," Rizzoli mutters beside me.

I slip it back in my pocket. "Sorry."

Word around the office is that he picked me only because I'm the youngest tech guy at Tranidek, meaning I'm the most camera friendly. But that didn't stop him from bringing in someone to put together my wardrobe for the event. It's all about appearances, right?

"Won't happen again," I tell him.

"Good."

I can't help but wonder whether the real reason I'm here is because Carlo told Rizzoli that I'm Fuse. This could be his way of making sure Olympia's man in black doesn't show up and ruin the ceremony. If Carlo is as paranoid as Dean says he is, he'll take extra precaution to make sure I'm still on his leash. Especially if he *is* the one behind Cale's disappearance like I suspect.

After ordering from the makeshift bar area, I take my plastic cup of water back to the standing table Rizzoli's at. He checks his watch and then locks eyes with Wallace for a moment.

"Waiting for something?" I ask.

He turns back to me. "Just for it to start. Should be any minute now."

The exchange between two of Martelli's men reminds me of the shootout I broke up the other night. Based off of my descriptions, Dean thinks that some of the men worked for his father. He figures they were retaliating for Luca's death, a move Carlo views as an attack on his empire. And despite the fact that I told Dean how his renewed relationship with his father makes me nervous, he's been to see Carlo three times this week. First Carlo needed to see Dean to make sure he was properly armed in case of an attack from Bello or his men, then he wanted to inform Dean of what areas of the city to stay out of—because that couldn't have been handled over the phone, apparently. Last night…well, I didn't really get an excuse from Dean.

I down my water and fix the sleeves of my suit.

"Sir, I don't mean to be disrespectful, but if you brought me to talk to reporters, shouldn't we go talk to them?" I ask.

He looks me over. "No. They're all busy talking to other people at the moment. But I did think more of them would've approached us by now."

"Excuse me, Mr. Rizzoli," a woman says as she walks over to our table. She's wearing black pants that blow in the breeze and a fluffy green jacket.

Rizzoli immediately stands up straighter.

"Mind if we ask you a few questions?" Another man wearing thick-framed glasses and carrying a camera with the WRBD logo on it squeezes through the crowd to our table. It's a competing station to the one Cale worked at.

"Absolutely," my boss answers.

"Okay, well the big news for Tranidek Energy—and the city, really—is your agreement with Wyatt Industries to split the solar roadways project. Can you tell us a little about Tranidek's technology and how the installation is going?"

"We're very excited to finally be implementing and installing the technology we've been working on for months," Rizzoli says in his practiced voice. He slaps my back and hooks his arm around my shoulder. "Ethan Pierce here is actually one of our newest software developers. He was thrown right into the deep end on his first day and picked it up right away."

The reporter pushes the microphone in my face. "What exactly are you doing for Tranidek, Mr. Pierce?" The WRBD logo is also on the front of her jacket.

"Uh, I was doing software development when I first started, but now that we've moved on to the installation part of the process, I've been out on the streets once in a while with our construction guys to verify that each solar panel we install is fully optimized."

Damn, I sound pretty smart.

"We want to ensure the accuracy of our services to our

customers," Rizzoli continues as the mic is quickly shifted up to him. "It's why we have people like Mr. Pierce out in the field to double-check that everything works."

"Could you—" The reporter notices someone else in the crowd and turns back to us. "Thank you so much for your time. Mr. Mayor!" She and her cameraman follow the crowd to Mayor Eugene Banks, who seems to have just arrived in a black limousine.

Rizzoli grumbles, and as they step away, I spot Myra.

"Ethan!" She worms her way to us.

"You made it!" I smile and give her a hug. Apparently that's what we do now. Ever since Cale disappeared, that is. "You look great."

What a difference from last week. Her curly hair is pulled up in a bun on the top of her head, and her eyes look bolder with fresh makeup. Over her blue dress she wears a white jacket, which she pulls tighter around her in the chill breeze.

She looks down. "Oh, thanks. I know I'm kind of late, but it took longer to get out of the office than I thought."

I feel a heavy hand on my shoulder and Rizzoli says to me, "Ethan, this man has some questions about our solar panels."

Shaking hands with a man with scruffy facial hair, I say, "Hi, I'm Ethan Pierce."

"Lester Coltman, *Olympia Tribune*." He looks to Myra.

"This is Myra Connors," I add quickly.

"Oh, I know." He smiles and shakes her hand. "I have some questions for you in a minute, if you don't mind."

"Not at all," she says, though I can hear the apprehension in her voice.

He turns back to me and Rizzoli. "Now, Tranidek Energy scored a major victory when you guys were able to split the solar roadways contract with Wyatt Industries. However, this new technology has recently been criticized for potential safety risks." He holds a recorder up to me. "Do you care to comment?"

"Uh…" I start, ever so eloquently, but Rizzoli leans over to speak for me.

"Through studies we've completed, we're certainly aware of

the potential driving risks that still exist. However, we're confident in our staff to perform a thorough job, from creation to installation to maintenance. It's because of these experts, like Mr. Pierce"—he motions to me—"that we don't see the risk being any greater than the inherent risk of getting in a moving vehicle driving on any surface."

"Skeptics claim that the solar roadways that are currently in use have been known to malfunction, confusing drivers with changing street lines or even cracking under the weight of certain vehicles. Are you taking any precautions to prevent issues of this kind moving forward?"

"The first roadways that were developed and installed by Tranidek were just laid down last week," Rizzoli continues. So much for bringing me to talk tech. "I believe those instances you're speaking of are with the Wyatt Industries–installed roadways, which were the first of their kind. I'm sure Wyatt is well aware of the glitch and will soon address those issues, per their contract with the city." He claps his hand down hard on my shoulder. "As for our precautions, I'll let Mr. Pierce tell you the steps we're taking to ensure efficiency."

They both look at me expectantly and my mind immediately goes blank.

Apparently, Rizzoli sees me stammer and adds, "Mr. Pierce was just out in the field last week alongside our laborers."

"Right," I say quickly as my brain returns to me. "I've been double-checking each panel for faulty ones to make sure they all work okay. We can keep track of their strength remotely afterward, but they need to be perfect when they're installed."

"And Tranidek started installing on Flint Parkway, correct?"

I nod, but Frank Rizzoli leans over to say, "Yes, between Main Street and Ashland Avenue."

"Any particular reason why you chose one of the wealthiest neighborhoods in the city to start?"

Without missing a beat at the accusations behind Coltman's words, Rizzoli responds, "Midtown West may be one of the wealthiest areas, but it also has some of the straightest, simplest, and least-traveled streets in the city. The clean street lines make installation easy while we're still at the beginning stages of implementation. Once our crews fully understand how to install the panels properly, we'll move on to the older, busier parts of the city with narrower and more complicated streets."

"Thank you, Mr. Rizzoli," Coltman says before turning his attention to Myra. "Now, Miss Connors, your career has certainly changed a lot in the last few months. You went from a councilman's assistant to a member of the council yourself. What has been the biggest challenge in your new role?"

The scrutiny, I think to myself.

"Really, it's just been restoring order to the mess my predecessor left behind. Going through everything with a fine-toothed comb: budgets, proposals, codes, everything. Just to make sure that we're following city and state laws while also doing our best to provide for the residents because, after all, they're really the ones I work for."

"What are your plans for the increased gang violence in your district?" Coltman asks.

"Well, like I said, I've been going through everything with a fine-toothed comb, and what I've discovered is that crime is actually down in Olympia."

"You don't think crime is an issue in Hopman?"

She shakes her head. "That's not exactly what I said. The overall crime rate may be down across the whole city, but the Hopman district continues to have the highest number of crimes, particularly violent crimes. However, in the short while I've been in this position, I can tell that it's not because of the residents living there. As we're all well aware from the case I brought to the city council and Olympia Police against Frank Lloyd and Michael Bello in November, this city has a major issue with organized crime. With the poverty levels of my district, it's no wonder that Hopman is hit the hardest."

"So you're saying the problems with your district are solely related to the mafia?" Coltman asks.

I can feel Rizzoli step closer behind me, but I don't dare turn to look at him.

"Not solely," Myra responds, "but it'd be interesting to see what would happen to the crime levels if the city was rid of this negative influence."

"Based off pictures printed in the *Tribune* last November, it appears you're good friends with Olympia's vigilante, Fuse. Any chance you'll ask him for help with the city's organized crime issue?"

She smiles brightly, although I know she's cursing him out in her head. "No. The accusations of me working with Fuse are completely false. The photos that were illegally printed in your newspaper insinuated something much worse than what was reality, which was me simply telling him that I had called security and that he'd be arrested for breaking into city hall."

"Judging from your position in the pictures—obtained legally, I might add—you seemed pretty casual to be telling him he's about to be arrested."

"Thank you for coming," Mayor Eugene Banks says from the podium.

"Miss Connors, just one more question," Coltman pushes.

She points to Mayor Banks. "Looks like it's starting. Thank you."

Coltman clicks off his microphone and moves closer to the podium to snap pictures.

"When Montgomery Works moved out of Olympia, this area of the city was left forgotten, neglected," Mayor Banks starts. "But today, I'm proud to say that, thanks to efforts by some of the most hardworking Olympians in the city, this area will no longer be forgotten…"

The rest of his speech is more or less hype for Wallace and the project. He drones on for what seems like forever, talking about how the project will be a boost to the neighborhood, provide opportunities for low-income families, and create jobs. He dances around the funding for the site—largely provided by state grants, tax breaks, and "private donations."

When he's done, he invites Leon Wallace to the podium to polite applause.

"Thank you, Mayor Banks. This project has been a passion of mine for some time now. After my first successful real estate investment many years ago, I've had my eye on this piece of property. Today, I'm proud to—"

Several members in the front of the crowd gasp and back away, pushing into me and Myra, forcing us to collide with the people behind us. I move up on my tiptoes, my leather shoes digging into my feet, and try to get a better look. All I can see is Wallace's horror-struck face as he looks to the edge of the crowd. Some people start running. Others scream. But Myra and I stay planted where we are as we watch in panicked curiosity.

Two men in suits run up to the podium, seizing Wallace by the arms and attempting to pull him away. That's when I spot Fizz step closer, only a few feet away from Wallace and the two other men. The creature opens his mouth and groans, shooting his deadly saliva in their direction. The crowd shouts louder than before, and everyone who hasn't already run away really starts to panic now. The gathering becomes a frenzy as the two men beside Wallace fall to the pavement, their arms burning with Fizz's venom.

When Myra is pushed to the ground, I tear my eyes away from the scene to make sure she's okay. All around us, people run in different directions, tripping on potholes or other people. I spot Coltman snapping pictures of Fizz, getting as close as he dares.

After I help Myra up, most of the crowd is gone. Fizz and Coltman are the only ones standing by the podium, and when Fizz hisses, the reporter takes several steps backward and trips over a pothole.

Slowly the creature steps toward me and Myra. Wallace and his two security men are on the ground, smoke—or maybe steam—rising from where they lay.

Myra grips my arm tight as Fizz moves closer to us, and I'm not sure if he's going to kill us next. I open my palm in his direction just in case. When he's finally close enough for me to see his eyes, though, I know he won't touch us.

The person staring back at me is my brother.

Chapter Six

Cale stares at us for a minute, Myra's hand clamped to my arm just above my elbow, and then turns away and shuffles back deeper into the complex. I consider going after him, but Coltman might follow me.

Looking over, though, I see his camera is hanging around his neck as he clutches his ankle.

"You okay?" I ask Myra.

She's shaken up, but nods. I wonder if she saw the same thing I did. Even if she did, it doesn't mean she believes it.

I rush over to Coltman. "Are you okay?"

"Not really. I think I messed up my ankle when I tripped. Don't even know if I got a good shot."

I glance down at the camera hanging around his neck as the sound of police sirens grow louder. "Well, just hang in there."

"Ethan, are *you* okay?" Myra asks when I return to her.

Cale disappeared into one of the buildings. After him being gone so long, to see him again—as a mutant, no less—doesn't seem real. But at the same time, I *know* it was him. But how did he end up like that? And why is he killing people?

Fuse: Oblivion

By time the police are ready to question us, the area has been taped off, and Coltman and a few others are being treated outside the back of an ambulance. Myra is wrapped in a blanket one of the officers brought over. He's the one who takes our initial statements. By the time we finish, I spot Tucker duck under the tape as he approaches.

He beelines right for us. "You two okay?"

Myra and I both nod.

"You're not hurt or anything?" he asks.

She shakes her head. "Just kind of jittery."

Tucker nods. "Yeah, I can imagine. So they're thinking it was that Fizz guy?"

"It was," I say. "He was standing five feet away from us."

"And his spit was like acid or something," Myra adds.

He puts his hands on his hips and scans the scene.

"Do you know why he looks like that?" Myra asks. "His skin was…" She shivers.

He shakes his head. "Unfortunately, we don't really know anything about him. Did you two already give your statements?"

We nod in unison again.

"Okay, well if you don't need any medical attention, you're free to go," he tells us. "If you remember anything, give me a call."

"We will." I'm not sure how honest I'm being with that. I hope that Cale was able to get far enough away that the police *can't* find him. I don't want them to hurt him. Or worse, him to hurt them. I don't know if he can control whatever is coming out of his mouth. I'd like to think he isn't choosing to hurt people, but I'm not convinced.

"Why don't you stay under the heater where it's warm, and I'll call us a cab," I tell her.

She nods, and I step out from under the tent and pull out my phone. There's a text from Rizzoli asking if I'm okay and telling me that I can take the rest of the day off, but to be in first thing in the morning. Honestly, I'm surprised I even got that much. After replying to Rizzoli, I immediately call Dean.

"Ethan! Are you okay?" He sounds a little worried. "I heard about the attack."

"Yeah, I'm fine. Wallace and two of his bodyguards are dead, though. Luckily, everyone else escaped with only sprained ankles and a couple scrapes and stuff."

"I've only heard bits and pieces from what's online," he says. "Someone said there was a gunman, another person said it was Fizz."

"It was Fizz, yeah." I kick at a loose chunk of pavement. Better to leave out what I saw in Fizz's eyes. I want to get more evidence first. Dean will think I'm crazy.

"Do you want me to see if I can reschedule my appointments for this afternoon?" he asks. "We can see if we can pick up a trail or something. Finally nab this freak."

I scrunch my nose at that. "No, you should stay at work. I think it's probably a good idea if I spend the day with Myra anyway. She'll say she's fine, but with everything with Cale—"

"Yeah, that makes sense," Dean says.

"I'll see if I can dig up anything on Fizz and then maybe we'll check this place out tonight."

"Okay, sounds good. I'm really glad you're okay, Ethan."

I smile and kick at the pavement chunk again. "Thanks, Dean."

———

"WHAT ARE WE even doing here?" Dean asks. "Wouldn't this Fizz guy be far away from here by now?"

"Shh," I hiss as we move on to the third derelict building in the Works complex.

The little research I managed to do on my phone while I was supposed to be watching a movie with Myra at her apartment didn't yield much. I found a few posts on social media that confirm that Fizz was spotted before he killed those men by the lake, but since they referred to him as "bigfoot," it's clear they didn't get a good look at him. No pictures, either.

There isn't much to see at the Works now that the sun's gone down. The empty brick warehouses are dark, damp, and dirty, each one worse than the last. Some remaining pieces of equipment and office furniture are still scattered about, but mostly this place is just a shell of what it used to be. It's going to take awhile to find Cale in a mess like this.

But I have to. Despite the ceremony ending up in total chaos and murder, seeing a glimpse of my brother gave me hope.

The problem is, even if he is my brother, is he still the same person? He killed those men by the water, Luca Martelli, and Leon Wallace and his men. Possibly even more that I don't know about. Did he mean to do it? Was it just for revenge? Is it over now? He didn't seem to care that he sprayed those guards who jumped on Wallace today. That's not like Cale. Maybe I didn't see him in Fizz like I thought. Maybe Cale really is dead and I'm putting myself and Dean in danger by being out here.

No, I know what I saw. Fizz is definitely Cale. But if I'm going to convince Dean—and I'm going to need his help to track down Fizz—I have to find concrete evidence to prove I'm right.

"What are we supposed to be looking for?" He whispers to me.

"Just anything…weird."

"And avoid the police outside at the same time? Sure, no problem."

"Shh."

The frenzy may have died down, but I know the police will still be scavenging evidence before it goes cold. And while I may be hidden behind my Fuse mask, Dean isn't. He may have been able to explain away Alexander using his apartment but creeping around another crime scene would look suspicious.

We move up to the former office space on the second floor. Peeling paint, graffitied walls, papers scattered all over the floor. This place is a mess. A few windows are broken, which has let in leaves and other debris from outside through the years. If there are any clues on where Cale might be now so I can talk to him and show Dean that he needs our help, this is where we'll find them.

"Are you sure this place is even safe?" Dean asks.

"Relax."

He huffs but doesn't offer a further retort.

Chapter Six

After we've searched the other rooms on the second floor—which look much like the first one—Dean moves toward the exit on the ground floor in the cavernous warehouse part of the building. I'm anxious to get out of here, especially as the blue lights reflect in the upper windows.

"Next building, then?" he asks.

I take in the former plant. It feels like there's still more here, but we've covered everything in this building. At least, as much as we could see.

"Do you think there's a basement?" I ask.

"I don't know. Maybe. Why?"

"Well, you told me yourself that people like your father usually get rid of people in hard-to-find places."

He narrows his eyes. "Is that what this is about?"

My cheeks flush.

"Ethan, even if we do find your brother, it's been four months. Are you sure you even want to find what's left of him?"

I was hoping to find a clue or something before he figured it out. Maybe I should've come by myself, but I've grown so accustomed to having him by my side as Fuse.

"I know. But we haven't found a body yet and I just thought—"

Something on the other end of the room crashes and we both duck out of sight between two large rusty toolboxes. There's little space behind them, barely enough room for both of us. It's uncomfortable, but I don't dare move. Even as the spiders crawl up my leg.

My heart pounds in my stomach as I wait for whoever made the noise to come into view. Maybe it was a cop. Or one of Martelli's men. Or a squatter. Which is the better of the three?

After a while of silence, I look over at Dean and mutter quietly, "I'm going to check it out."

Trying to keep as low as possible, I move slowly along the wall to the source of the noise. All the way to the corner and still no sign of anybody. Standing up straight, I look around.

Something moves across my foot, and I look down to see a rat run along the concrete floor.

I shout and jump, backing into a large piece of metal, causing it to fall to the floor with a loud clang.

Dean runs up looking worried. "You okay?"

"It was a rat."

He breaks into a smile and doubles over laughing. "So much for stealth!"

"Shut up," I throw a punch at him halfheartedly, but he swats it away. Behind me, I notice the piece of metal I dropped was covering a door. "Think I found the basement."

The wooden door is half-rotten. The bottom of it looks like it's splattered in a murky brown substance. I don't even want to think about what it could be.

The door doesn't take much effort to open since it's so deteriorated. The doorknob literally pulls away from the door in my hands.

"Help me out," I tell Dean.

We wedge the door open, crumbling more of it onto the concrete floor in the process. The strong smell of fumes hit us once the door is open. Dean turns away with a sour look on his face.

"Ugh, what is that?" He lifts his shirt above his nose.

I pinch my nose with my fingers. "I don't know." I take in the metal staircase and spot a piece of purple fabric on the first step. I kneel down and pick it up carefully. It looks like it's about to disintegrate.

"What's that?" Dean asks.

The corner of the Olympia University logo is stitched in with white thread. My heart rate quickens.

"I think this is Cale's." I don't care what Dean thinks right now. I need to say it out loud to make it real. Besides what I saw today, this is the first real clue I have that shows what happened to my brother.

"How do you figure?"

"He had an OU shirt *just* like this!"

"Ethan, do you know how many students are enrolled in OU? How many alumni? You, for instance."

I shake my head. "No, look, the logo is stitched. That was what student advocators wore, which Cale was during his senior year."

"Okay, that narrows down the list, but it doesn't mean it's Cale's."

I shoot him a look. Even through my mask he gets the message.

He puts up his hands in surrender. "I'm just playing devil's advocate right now. I don't want you to get your hopes up."

"Well, I'm convinced. Cale wore this shirt a lot."

"Okay, so let's say it's his. What's it doing here?"

I look down at the step I found the fabric on. It looks about as trustworthy as the door.

"I'm not going down there," Dean declares.

Looking back at him with a smirk, I ask, "Scared?"

"Says the person who just screamed like a girl because of a rat."

The putrid smell and the crumbled door make me hesitate. The plant didn't close that long ago. The door couldn't have been that rotted, could it? But if Cale was here, I have to check it out.

Crouching down, I try to get a good look from where I stand, but it's too dark. "I need a flashlight or something."

"I only have a gun," Dean replies. "Usually we're not trying to draw attention to ourselves with lights."

I ignore him and hand over the fabric.

Carefully, I move to the first step. The smell hits me harder. Like sulfur and fumes mixed together.

Dean grabs my shoulder and pulls me back before my foot makes contact. "Hey, you don't have to do this." There's a hint of worry in his voice.

"Just a couple steps." I move down two steps, gripping the handrail tightly. Even if I wanted to go all the way down, I couldn't. Murky fluid fills the basement at least a foot deep, maybe even two.

That must be what Cale was looking for. Proof that the Works isn't safe. I half wonder if there's anything else down here worth seeing. Something that would convince Dean that Cale really was here.

Taking one more step, I only register how soft it is just as it gives way. I grab on to the handrail, which also breaks away. My hands grasp for the next sturdy surface I can reach, scratching at the rough concrete wall until I catch something sturdy and steady myself.

"Ethan!" Dean shouts and takes the two steps down to pull me back up.

Once I'm on the concrete floor in the main room, he examines my injuries.

"You okay?" He grabs my arms and looks at my bleeding hands. Nothing too bad.

I nod. "Yeah. I'm fine."

"What'd you see?"

"Some sort of chemical waste pit down there. The whole basement's filled with it."

"Guess Cale was right with his story," he says.

"Which would be even more reason for your father to kill him."

"Ethan…"

"No, Dean, there's a fucking chemical vat in the place Cale was about to expose for health threats. Someone from *your* family must've thrown him in there! Cale's Fizz, Dean. It just makes sense. God only knows what's down there and what it could do to him!"

"Wait a minute, back up. You think Cale is Fizz?"

"I know he is."

"And you think my father is the one who threw him into the pit down there?"

"Probably not him personally. I would say that Wallace had more to do with it, but I'm sure your father welcomed the idea."

Dean sidesteps my comment and asks, "So you think he mutated or something?"

I shrug. "I don't really know. I guess that's as good an idea as any." Now that I think about it, though, it *does* sound likely.

"Ethan, that's ridiculous."

"Why? It happened to me. Maybe there's something in our DNA that makes us more likely to mutate during extreme circumstances than be harmed by them. I don't know. What I do know is that Fizz exists and he's hurting people. I believe it's

Cale, which means if we find him, we can talk him out of hurting anyone else."

"That's ridiculous. *If* your brother was thrown in there, he would be dead. Just take a look at this door! Besides, Myra said he went missing the night…*that* night."

I look away from him. Now's not the time to discuss that night.

"When would my father have had the chance?" he continues.

"I told you, he was gone for a long time before he met up with us."

Dean ignores me. "And why would my father kill him here when he knew there would be crews tearing this place down in a few months? His men usually just throw people from the top of Emerson Bluffs."

I think back to Aiden Lipinski and George Kingston. Their bodies were discovered there right after Carlo said he'd take care of them. But if Cale's body was found when it was known by his coworkers that he was investigating a shady development, it would spark a foul-play investigation.

Meanwhile, Carlo could've just had Cale killed here because he knew Leon Wallace's company was the one redeveloping the Works, meaning if any of the men stumbled upon my brother's body, they could be paid off or bribed to keep it quiet

"Ethan, I know you're looking for closure, but I really don't think you're going to find any." He puts his hand on my shoulder. "I'm sorry."

Chapter Seven

My world seems to be passing by in a blur. From the ride home to taking off the suit to plopping on the couch with a bottle of wine, none of it seems to last long in my memory. I'm so focused on Cale. The pain and sorrow I've been pushing away for the last four months hits me all of a sudden now that I know what's happened to him—no matter what Dean says to the contrary. I know what I saw. It was definitely Cale. The question is, how?

I polish off the bottle by myself within twenty minutes and only get up in order to grab another one. By the time I sit back down, my head is really spinning.

"Do you want something to eat?" Dean asks from the kitchen behind me. He didn't say anything when I grabbed the second bottle, but he was probably judging me. Whatever. At this moment, I don't really care.

I stare at the blank TV screen, too lost in my own thoughts. "Cale's never going to be the same again," I finally say.

He sighs. "Why's that?"

"You saw him." My eyes flicker up to his reflection in the

window. He's leaning against the counter facing my direction. "The way he looks now. You saw what he can do. You saw the shit they threw him in to make him that way."

My mind goes crazy imagining how terrified Cale must've been. How much pain he was probably in. My hatred for Leon Wallace and Carlo Martelli and all of them resurfaces. First Emma, now Cale.

And to think, I was happy to see Carlo that night that everything happened. The night Dean and I were almost sliced up by a sadistic pervert. Carlo saved us that night, but he also probably turned my brother into the monster he is now. My stomach turns at the memory.

"Ethan, he's not—"

"I don't know how I'm going to explain this to my parents," I say, not really listening to him. "They already think I'm stepping into a battlefield every time I walk out of the apartment. At this point, they're not exactly wrong. After they hear about Cale, they're going to lose their shit. Mom especially."

Dean finally relents to me not backing down from thinking—from *knowing*—that Cale is Fizz and comes to sit beside me on the couch.

I take another big gulp straight from the bottle. Half gone already. "They're not going to believe me. They'll call me crazy. They'll probably even think it's a side effect of me getting electrocuted last year."

"I don't think they'll think that. They'll be confused, sure, but they're not going to outcast you. Not after they just lost your brother."

"Maybe." I circle my thumb over the rim of the bottle. "Myra is already a mess about everything. Not having Cale here is really crushing her spirit. If she knows Cale's still out there, even if he's not the same person…"

Another swig. Only a quarter of the bottle left now. A proper glass of wine. I should share it with Dean, but I keep the bottle locked in my hand.

"I wonder if Cale is even still Cale…"

"What do you mean?" he asks.

"Does he remember anything from when he was human? When he was only my brother? Does he even remember me? Myra? That he loves her? That he was going to propose to her? That he was normal once?"

"I don't think he'd ever forget any of that," Dean says. "Especially you guys."

"He looked at us today. Stared right at us after he killed Wallace. He had to recognize us." I shake my head and the room spins. "But Cale wouldn't ever kill anyone. It's not who he is, so why would he do it as Fizz? Even if he does remember who tried to kill him…"

I expect Dean to try to convince me that Cale isn't Fizz. That he's dead and Fizz is someone else. But he doesn't. Instead, he pulls the bottle away from me and sets it on the coffee table.

"You need some water." He goes to the kitchen and runs the faucet. My eyes remain fixed on my reflection in the TV. When Dean retakes his seat, he passes the glass to me. "You should probably eat something too. I know it's late, but we haven't had a proper meal. I can make something real quick or call for a pizza."

"No, I'm fine," I tell him.

We sit in silence as I sip my water. Already I can feel my head clearing a bit, but I'm still groggy. Still exhausted. Still sad from discovering Cale's fate. I have to do something to help. At the very least, get him to stop killing people. Even if they are Martelli's men.

Maybe Wes can think of something to save him. Bring the Cale I know back. Without any side effects.

My head nods as my eyelids grow heavy.

"Come on." Dean gets up and offers his hands. "If you're not going to eat, you should go to bed. You're falling asleep as it is. You'll feel better in the morning."

Setting my glass aside, he grabs my hands and pulls me up. The room spins faster, and I realize how much the wine has really hit me. I step toward my bedroom and bump into the side of the couch.

Dean quickly puts his hand on me to steady me. "You good?"

"I'm okay," I tell him, but his hand remains where it is as

we move toward my bedroom. I look at him and say, "I can get myself ready for bed."

"Okay. I'll get you another glass of water, though, for the morning."

When he leaves, I undress and crawl into bed. He comes in a minute later with a fresh glass of water that he sets on the nightstand.

"Need anything else?" he asks.

I move over and pat the bed. "Come here."

He sits on the edge with a smirk. "What?"

"I really appreciate you, you know?" My voice squeaks at the end of the sentence and I giggle. The full effects of the alcohol are taking over now, and drunk Ethan is talking. "You take such… good care of me. Even when I'm an asshole." My lips pucker as I draw out each word.

He chuckles. "No problem."

"Hey, you're awesome." I point at him animatedly and roll closer to him. "You're one of a kind, Dean."

His smile grows wider. "Oh yeah? Why's that?"

"You make me feel…all sorts of things. Weird things. You're the only man I'll ever be attracted to. And, if you're not ready for this"—my mouth stretches to a lion's yawn—"good lovin', that's okay. I'll wait. You're worth it." I pat his leg as my eyes drift closed.

His voice is subdued. "Thanks."

I reach up to his muscular arm and pull him closer to me until our lips meet. He puts his hand on the side of my face and leans into it for a moment before breaking it off. My hand lingers on his as he backs away until he's out of reach.

He clicks off the light and steps to the door. "Good night, Ethan."

———

MY HEAD ACHES this morning. The bright sun shining through the large window doesn't help either. I forgot to close the curtains last night, and this morning, of all mornings, is one of the sunniest this week. Ordinarily I'd be happy for the spring-time sun, but today I'd rather it was gloomy.

Tossing the blanket over my face, I roll over to try to sleep a bit longer, but my full bladder and dry throat force me out of bed. I should've had more than one glass of water. And probably should've listened to Dean last night and eaten something.

I'm definitely not twenty-one anymore.

Swinging my feet to the floor, I gulp down the glass of water on the nightstand. That helps a little bit.

"Morning," Dean says cheerfully from the kitchen counter. An empty cereal bowl sits next to the newspaper spread out in front of him.

I grunt at him as I pass by to the bathroom. When I come out, he's putting toast on a plate.

"Here, this will help." He slides the plate and a banana in front of me.

"More water," I croak in my early-morning voice.

Again, he smiles and fills a glass for me. "I've already been to the gym and done the dishes, and I was about to go in to work to catch up on some paperwork."

I nod as I nibble at my toast.

"You going to go for a run today?"

"I really don't feel like it," I say.

"You should. It'll get the blood flowing and probably get rid of your headache."

"It's going to be the slowest run I've been on since I started."

"At least you'll be moving."

"True." I replay the events of last night in my head and debate whether I should bring up what I told Dean. About being attracted to him. Internally I'm cringing about opening a door Dean didn't want to open. But drunk words are sober thoughts.

Besides, Dean and I have been dancing around our feelings for months now. After he said he needed space because of what happened with James Alexander, I respected that. He was depressed before, but he's slowly getting better. Back to his normal self. I'd like to think I've helped at least a little bit with that.

Other than work, we spend every second together. It's like

we're married without any physical relationship. And it's finally coming to the point where it's not enough for me. I want more from Dean, but if he still hasn't worked through what happened to him, I can't push it. I meant what I said last night. He's worth waiting for.

He folds up the paper and takes his bowl to the sink. His movement brings me back to reality.

"You heading out, then?" My voice is clearing up a little.

"In a minute. I want to talk to you first."

I feel lightheaded from nerves, but I try to play it off. "About what?"

He leans on the counter across from me. "I think you know."

"Oh."

"Yeah." He doesn't meet my eyes either.

"I was drunk."

"But you weren't lying."

My cheeks flush and I mutter, "No."

"Ethan, that kiss was…really nice."

"But…?" I know there's a but. Otherwise there wouldn't be a need for a discussion. Dean would've stayed last night if he wasn't having doubts.

"We can't do this. Not yet, at least. I'm just not there yet."

"Oh."

"You said you were going to wait for me, and I believe that you would, but I can't ask you to do that."

"You're not." Now I look up at him.

He lets out a deep breath as he studies me a moment. "I still care a lot about you, and I hope someday soon I will be ready to be with someone, but I still need some time to figure out my own stuff for now."

I nod, disappointed. I know I shouldn't be. I was preparing myself for this. But I thought maybe things were different.

"Right now, the way things are between us…it works. Let's not rush anything."

The problem is, it doesn't work. Not completely. Not for me, at least. When we're out in the field doing Fuse stuff, sure, we work. But at home, it doesn't. Not anymore.

I look down at my plate and brush the crumbs off my fingers. "Okay."

"Are you okay? Are we good?" He leans down to try to catch my eyes.

Looking up at him, I lie, "Yeah. We're good."

"Good." He watches me for a minute.

"What?" I ask.

"There's something else."

"What?" My heart pounds in my chest.

He turns the paper to me and I read the headline: *"Bello no longer in police custody."*

"What!" I say for the third time.

"He killed the men who were supposed to be watching him and took off. The car he stole was left at a truck stop an hour out. Probably took a bus or something before he tried to steal another car."

"You think he's coming back here?"

Dean shrugs. "Could be. It's hard to say. On the one hand, he probably wants to avoid being arrested again, but on the other, he definitely has some unfinished business here."

"What do you mean? He already told the police all about your father's operations."

"Yeah, and it didn't have the effect he expected. He wanted my father's empire to crumble. The police haven't moved in on anyone yet."

"Why not?"

"That's a question for your cop friend."

I cover my mouth as I stare at the headline again. I'll have to give Tucker a call. Maybe he'll have time to get lunch or something. Then again, if Bello is on the loose, he's probably busy. Even if he's known for a while, he'll be tied up dealing with the press. It's worth a shot, though.

"Well, I should get going," Dean finally says. "What are you doing today? Just hanging around?"

"No." I lean back and run my hand through my matted hair to pull myself out of our conversation. "I want to take a sample of the acid we found yesterday and give it to Wes. Maybe he can test it to see if it matches what the coroner found on Luca's body. If it does, at least we know where it came from. Probably who did it, too."

Dean nods. "Be careful. Call me if you need anything."

"Will do. See you later."

After Dean leaves, I start to miss him. Usually we go to the gym in the morning, which is an hour or two that we're together before we go to work. Nothing of significance, just time together.

It's stupid. If I wanted him to come with me to the Works, I should've said something. How else is he going to know? But he made it clear that he wants to be just friends right now. I have to accept that.

A part of me is embarrassed for putting myself out there last night, but at least it's out in the open now. I know for sure where things stand between us. Where Dean's head's at.

Besides, I have other things to worry about. Like Bello returning, and figuring out what exactly happened to Cale. My brother's mystery starts with the sample. It's all just to cover my bases to make sure I'm doing my due diligence. I'm already convinced Fizz is Cale.

Honestly, I'm hoping to see him when I get the sample. If I can get him alone, maybe I can talk to him. See how much of Cale is in there and what I can do to help him. Hopefully there's a chance he can return to normal.

———

I HOLD AN empty glass jar in my gloved hands as I move through the Works complex. Even though it's in the middle of the afternoon, I still put on my Fuse suit. Can never be too careful, especially when the police are probably still searching the Works for Fizz.

This place is actually pretty quiet now that I'm inside. Some policemen were grouped around the main entrance where the ground-breaking ceremony took place, but I slipped past them into one of the buildings in the back of the complex and meandered my way through.

Fuse: Oblivion

With the police focus on the Works thanks to Fizz's latest attack, it's probably best for me to go straight to the basement, take the sample, and get out, but I want to do a little more exploring. I'm hoping the sunlight will let me see anything Dean and I might've missed last night.

The complex is more mazelike than I realized. I know all the buildings are connected to each other, but finding those connections is more difficult than I thought.

As I turn another corner and see the warehouse with the chemical pit through a smashed window, I realize I'm lost. I can't figure out how to get over there. The building I'm in is open like the warehouse with the chemical pit, but all along the top floors are doorways leading to smaller rooms. Probably private offices or something, but maybe one of the doors leads to a catwalk to the next building.

After I find a staircase in the corner and make my way up to the second floor, I step carefully on the walkway next to the offices, glancing inside each room to see what's there. Mostly there's just scattered papers blown on the floor or glass from a smashed-in window. Three of the offices still have the furniture inside, like someone forgot to clean it out on their last day of work.

I find the door that leads to the hallway into the next building but hesitate when I grab the doorknob. The door to the room at the end of the hall is closed. All the other doors were open except for the one leading to the next building and the one at the end of the hall.

I step down the hallway and open the door, wishing I had brought Dean with me. Although this room looks just as disheveled as the other offices, it's clearly still being used. I set the glass jar down on the floor and step inside. A tarp hangs over the window, casting a blue glow over the room. A dirty jacket sits in the corner, along with several worn newspapers laid flat and taped together like a makeshift blanket.

What catches my eye, though, is the newspaper clippings stuck to the walls. I spot Myra in one and step closer to read it. *"Connors elected newest council member."* Just below it is a story about her voting against the Works project. Next to it is an interview she did with the paper during her first week in office.

The next wall over is filled from floor to ceiling with stories about the Martellis, specifically Michael Bello and the Works redevelopment. From Bello's plea deal all the way to Fizz's attack at the ground-breaking ceremony—

The air seems to be sucked from my lungs. This must be where he sleeps. This is where Cale lives now. Based on the way he's kept up on everything that the Martellis are doing in the city, he must be angry. The men who did this to him are still walking, breathing, scheming. Meanwhile he's been left for dead.

I could stay here and read through these articles and try to see the world through Cale's eyes, but that wouldn't solve anything. I know where he's living. I know where to find him so I can talk to him. Right now, I need to get the sample and get it to Wes.

———

HOLDING THE GLASS jar of acid in my hand, I wait for Wes to call me back to his office at the clinic. Luckily, there aren't a lot of people here right now.

"Mr. Pierce, how are you?" Wes steps into the waiting room and shakes my hand. "Come on back." He leads me down the fluorescent-lit hallway to the small office. "What brings you in?"

"You remember what I texted you about the other day?" I ask.

"Oh, I'm sorry! I meant to do some preliminary research and get back to you about that, but I got busy with other things, and it honestly just slipped my mind."

"That's okay. I have something that's sort of related but… well, it's kind of weird."

"I'd expect nothing less." He chuckles as he closes the door behind us. "What do you have there?"

I set the jar on the counter. "This is a highly acidic mixture I got from the Works. There was a whole pool of this stuff in the basement of one of the buildings."

Wes picks it up and examines its murky greenish-brown color. "Interesting. Evidently the rumors of the high levels of toxicity still present in that complex are true."

"You heard about that?"

"I'm familiar with a few folks who work in environmental sciences at the university, and they've shared their skepticism about the cleanup of the waste produced by the Montgomery Works Company."

"Well, this is proof. I was kind of hoping you or Alex could test it to see what's in it."

"Oh. As I've said, we've been quite busy, Ethan."

"Please? This is really important. I'm hoping you can figure out what this is and what effects it could have on someone."

"What is this for?" He sets the jar back down.

"You've heard of this Fizz guy, right?"

He nods. "Is that why you were asking about mutants? Have you encountered him as Fuse?"

"Yeah. I'm willing to bet he mutated after being submerged in chemicals at the Works." I point to the jar.

"What makes you say that?"

"Well, he shoots acid out of his mouth and…" I trail off and consider how I'm going to explain myself so he doesn't think I'm crazy. If he dismisses me right away, he'll put off getting the sample tested. "Dean and I went to the morgue to look at a body that was probably killed by Fizz. The coroner listed a bunch of chemicals present on the body. If they match what's in that jar, we know where Fizz came from."

He nods and examines the jar again. "I see."

"You probably think I'm nuts."

He takes in a deep breath and crosses his arms. "Well, I have to be honest, I am a bit skeptical about your theory. If this mixture is as deadly as you claim it is, there's no way anyone could've survived being submerged in it. If it is, in fact, the same substance found on Fizz's victims, any contact with skin would likely burn it away. This is all just guesswork, of course. We have yet to study the sample."

Right. He thinks I'm crazy. I'll have to go back to Cale's

hideout and ask him how he became this creature. Hopefully I don't get my face burned off in the process. If he really is my brother, I'll be fine. If he's not...

"Could you guys please study it anyway?" I ask.

Wes nods again. "I'll see what I can do. I still have my doubts, but you have my attention. After what I discovered with your own mutation and what you're able to do with it, I guess anything is possible."

Chapter Eight

Dean said he was on his way home two hours ago but I still haven't seen him. I texted him an hour ago but haven't gotten a response, even though I've checked for one about a million times. My mind is going crazy wondering where he could be, fearing that he's suffered a fate similar to my brother's. I have half a mind to go out and look for him, but he could be anywhere. And what happens if I'm wrong?

Just as I consider calling him, I hear the staircase door bang down the hallway outside. Embarrassed for overreacting, I bury my face in my phone. I don't want to show him just how worried I was.

"Hey," he says when he steps inside. "How'd everything go with Wes?"

"Good. He's going to test the sample."

He pours himself a glass of water. "That's good."

"Yeah."

Taking a seat in the chair next to the couch, he asks, "So what else have you been up to today?"

I pause and debate whether I should bring up the fact that

he took so long to get home. But who am I to dictate when he needs to be home by?

"My meeting with Wes didn't take as long as I thought it would, so I listened to the police scanners in the basement of the clinic."

Dean takes a sip of his water. "Yeah? Did you find anything?"

I shake my head. "Not really. I ended up digging through outstanding arrest warrants and running the images through my facial recognition software."

"Anything good?"

"Turned in a guy who robbed a couple banks throughout the city."

"There you go," he says with a smile.

I turn my phone over and over in my hands, still thinking about the time between Dean leaving the office and when he walked through the door.

"You're home a little late, aren't you?" I finally say.

"Oh. Sorry about that. I, uh, ended up having to run an errand for my father."

"An errand? What kind of errand?" I can feel myself getting hotter with anger.

"Relax, I was just dropping off a package to a friend of his in the Lakeside Village."

"What kind of package?"

He shrugs. "I don't know."

"Who was the friend?"

"Ethan, what are you getting at?"

"This doesn't seem familiar to you?" I can't help but feel like Dean's being taken advantage of without him even realizing it. "You don't recognize the initiation pattern?"

"Initiation—what are you talking about? You think my father's trying to *recruit* me again?"

"That's what it looks like to me."

"He's my *father*, Ethan. I was doing him a *favor*. You can't just expect me to ignore him. Just like I know you're not going to let go of the idea that Cale turned into Fizz."

"Cale *did* turn into Fizz!"

"And based off of what he's been doing, I think we need to put a stop to him."

"What do you mean 'what he's been doing?'"

"He killed Wallace, who was on my father's side. Now that Bello's out, it's just further proof that he's building an army against my father. Fizz could be a part of that."

I roll my eyes and turn away. "Oh, come on."

"No, listen to me, Ethan: this Fizz guy—whether or not he's Cale—is dangerous. He's killing people!"

"He's killing Martellis, mostly," I correct.

"Still people."

"Since when do you care about the people who work for your father?"

"I grew up with a lot of them, okay? It's hard to ignore that history."

"So you're saying you'd rather protect them?"

He shakes his head. "That's not what I'm saying."

"But you want me to kill my brother."

"You want me to kill my father."

"I never said that."

"You didn't have to. You make it pretty obvious."

"I just don't want you to talk to him," I say. "I thought we both agreed on that, but then you're running errands for him, which is probably the start of the initiation process again."

"Ethan, it was just an errand!"

"Just one?"

He looks out the window.

"Dean..."

"Okay, it's been a few errands. Mostly after work. But it's not a big deal."

"Not a big—" I cut myself off. "Whatever. Apparently you're going to do what you want so what does it matter what we discuss?"

"And what about Fizz? Just because you think he's Cale, you're suddenly okay to look past the fact that he's killing people? Ethan, he needs to be stopped."

"Is that what Daddy Dearest wants? For you to use your

position with me to stop Fizz so Carlo can laugh in my face after I kill my own brother?"

"He has a point, Ethan. Fizz is dangerous."

"And Carlo isn't? Why is Fizz more dangerous than him? Is it just because Fizz is killing your father's people? Now all of a sudden killing is wrong when before your father wouldn't even bat an eye at killing off someone he disagreed with?"

"That's not—you're blowing this out of proportion!" he shouts.

"No, I think I have a pretty good handle on this. You're so desperate for your father's approval that you'll stoop as low as being his little bitch again. Never mind the fact that you and I—" I stop short. I've already said things I'll regret later.

"We what?" Dean asks. "We're not together. If I want to run a few errands for my father, I will. You don't have to know where I've been or what I'm doing."

All I can do is nod. After what I said last night, that stings. Apparently, he takes notice.

"Sorry," he says. "I didn't—that was out of line. Sorry."

I take a deep breath and try to start over. Arguing isn't going to solve anything. Not when the argument shifts to us as a couple. That's too close to the nerve.

"It's okay," I mutter.

"My father thinks Fizz broke into Joe Gotti's underground casino last week," Dean says. "After Luca and Leon, he's really paranoid."

"Wait a minute…Joe Gotti runs an underground casino? I thought he was Rizzoli's assistant?"

"He is. The casino is his side hustle. These men never stop trying to make money. And Gotti has a lot of it. Which is why my father is freaking out that he was broken into."

"Does he think Bello hired Fizz?"

"He *is* attacking my father's men specifically. After Leon Wallace, my father's not taking any chances."

I consider it for a moment. Would Cale work with Michael Bello, who was brought down by evidence Myra unearthed? Cale must've known what he had done. But maybe he's desperate enough for revenge that working with a man as horrible as Bello is the better option.

But that's not Cale. The chemicals might've changed his body, but I have to believe he's still in there. Revenge and stopping the Works project are his reasons for killing. He's not someone's hit man.

"Fizz is probably only attacking those men because they're tied to Cale's disappearance," I finally say.

"Ethan, it's my family that's dying. Fizz needs to be stopped. What if I'm next?"

"What about *my* family? Cale was just trying to expose the truth behind the Works, and they took him!"

"You don't know that!" Dean shouts.

"What about Cale's shirt?"

"You don't know for sure that it's his."

"Maybe not, but I also found where he's staying today."

Dean narrows his eyes. "What?"

"He's living in one of the buildings at the Works. He had newspaper clippings from the last four months on the Works, the Martellis, and Myra. Who else could it be?"

This seems to stop him. "Okay, so it might be Cale, but it doesn't mean my father had anything to do with it."

"Then tell me, how come it took your father almost an *hour* to get to Alexander's house that night? We almost died, Dean, because he was off trying to kill my brother."

He stiffens up at the mention of Alexander.

I continue in a softer tone. "Carlo said he went to your apartment to check out my story, but it shouldn't have taken him that long to get back to us. Something isn't adding up, and it's all pointing to him playing a major role in Cale's…disfigurement."

Dean's quiet for a moment, still staring at me with wild eyes. Finally, he blinks and looks down. "What I remember is my father helping us that night. So if you want to play the blame game, that's fine. Just don't expect me to be a part of it."

He gets up and snatches his keys from the counter.

"Where are you going?"

"Just leave me alone for now."

Chapter Eight

———

THE SMELL OF coffee wafts in the air as I fill a mug from the cupboard. To my surprise, when I called Tucker last night to see if he wanted to catch up, he said he could stop over this morning. We've been getting together every so often since Cale disappeared. His way of making sure I'm okay. I used to think it was completely unnecessary for him to check up on me, but now I've grown to enjoy our chats. Especially if I can get useful information out of him. I want to know if he knows anything about Cale that I don't know. Or Bello, now that he's free.

"So Dean's officially moved in to Cale's room then, huh?" Tucker asks when he emerges from the bathroom.

"Yeah, the room was just sitting empty, and Dean needed to get off the couch." I lean against the counter and set the coffee mug down.

Tucker takes a seat at one of the barstools and reaches for the mug. "So you're doing okay with Cale being…gone?"

I nod. "Yeah. I mean, I wish things were different, but there's no sense worrying about things you can't change."

"That's true. What about Myra? Have you talked to her since the incident at the Works?" He takes a careful sip.

"I spent the rest of that day with her, but otherwise not much." I go to the fridge to pour myself a glass of water. "We've texted a bit. She seems fine. More pissed than anything. I think it brings back bad memories from when she was spotted with Fuse a few months ago."

"I can imagine. First Fuse, now Fizz. Where are these guys even coming from?"

I lean forward on the counter, cradling my cool glass of water. "I don't know."

"This city is becoming a freak show."

"What do the police really know about this Fizz guy? Did they ever find him after he killed Leon Wallace?"

"That place is huge, so it's taking some time to really look through everything. There is one room we thought he might've been staying in, but it could just as easily be someone who's homeless."

"What did you find?" I ask.

"Oh, one of the empty offices had a stockpile of food. Canned goods, boxes of cereal, stuff like that."

Interesting. I wonder if Cale is occupying multiple rooms in case one of them is compromised.

"We're still searching it, though," Tucker adds.

"What do you think was his reason for killing Wallace?"

He snorts. "I don't know, but the pattern is the same as a few other murders. He leaves behind a chemical residue. It's hard to determine a motive. We know more about Fuse at this point. At least he seems to be *trying* to help the police."

Chills run up my arms. "What do you know about Fuse?"

"More educated guesses, really. He also has a pattern: his victims all show signs of electrocution—no matter how mild. Which is obvious since the guy runs around with a lightning bolt on his chest. He seems to be targeting gangs and some of Martelli's men, so that's good." He shrugs. "With all the crap going on nowadays, as long as he's not killing people, he's not our top priority. Sad that it's come to that."

"So you'd arrest him if you had the chance?"

"Hard to say. It'd be at the discretion of the arresting officer."

I nod to stop myself from asking any more questions. Can't have too many inquiries into Fuse.

"So everything's good here? You're doing okay?" He raises his mug to take a sip, but I know he's just trying to hide the worry on his face.

"Are you expecting a different answer than the one I just gave?" I grin, knowing he's only repeating himself because he wants to be sure.

"I just didn't know if you were still holding out hope that Cale is alive."

The smile falls from my face. "Oh. You never know, right?"

"I guess not, but I think it's important to prepare yourself for realistic outcomes."

My fingers tap against the cold glass in my hands. "My dad

thinks the same thing. He doesn't want me to talk about the possibility that Cale's still alive to my mom. Doesn't want to get her hopes up. I guess I can't blame him."

"What do you think happened to Cale?" he asks. "Honestly."

I know what happened to him and I'm still not sure how I feel about that.

"I don't know," I lie. "It seems coincidental that he disappeared just before he did his exposé on the Works, but you guys haven't found anything."

"And you know I'm doing all I can to find him, Ethan."

"Yeah, I know," I tell him with a nod.

"I know it's frustrating to not have any answers, but you'll get through it. As long as you and Myra and your parents are doing okay, that's what matters most right now."

"And we are. All doing okay, that is. Actually, now that Dean's moved in, it's not like I'm struggling with the bills, either."

"Mmm," he mumbles.

"What?"

"Can I ask you something?" He places his mug down on the counter and wipes away the ring from where it last sat. "I know we've discussed this a little bit before, but I just have this bad feeling, and if I've learned anything from this job, it's to trust my gut."

Swallowing hard, I mutter, "Sure."

"You trust Dean, right?"

"Absolutely."

"And you're sure he's not still in communication with his father or any other member of his family?"

"Yes," I say, looking him dead in the eyes. It's important to nail this. Tucker's job is to see through bullshit, which is entirely what I'm feeding him now. Dean's on my side. He may be talking to Carlo again—might even be obliviously starting an initiation process again—but I know sooner or later he'll come to his senses. Hopefully he'll realize that before anyone gets hurt.

I have to tell myself that so I don't go crazy with paranoia. After everyone I've lost, I need to have someone on my side. Besides, I care a lot about Dean. I need to protect him.

"How do you know?" Tucker asks.

"What do you mean?"

"How do you know he's not lying to you? He's a criminal."

"Not anymore. He was arrested a long time ago and has stayed away from his father ever since."

"And you're sure?"

"Yes. We're always together. When would he have time to talk with his father?"

"You're not with him now."

I turn my eyes away. Dean purposely left early this morning. Between our fight last night and Tucker coming today, there was no way he was going to stick around. Still, he didn't tell me where exactly he was going while Tucker's here.

I look back at him to keep my mind from wandering. Worrying.

"He's at the gym," I lie, though not as convincingly as I would like.

"Okay." He reaches for his coffee again.

"Since we're on the subject of Carlo Martelli, can I ask *you* a question?"

He smirks. "Sure."

"How are the police handling the mafia's influence in Olympia? Seems to me like they're only getting bigger, and the blame is being shoved onto Myra, who shouldn't be expected to have an answer for such a large problem so early in her position. And now Michael Bello's escaped police custody, so it doesn't seem like the police are doing much."

It all comes spewing out of me as if Tucker's the one to blame for Bello's escape or the way Myra's been treated in the press.

He looks at me with raised eyebrows. "Wow. That must've been building up for a while."

"It's just frustrating to watch someone with such good intentions be dragged through the mud. And then someone who's such a bastard gets away."

Tucker nods. "First of all, I agree that the *Tribune* has been very unfair to Myra. But it's a tough job. It's a bad district. A lot of people expect a lot of things from her, and she needs to be able to live up to those expectations to a degree. And second, I can guarantee that just because Bello is no longer in our custody, that doesn't mean he's getting what he wanted. Life on the run is no life at all. We'll find him. Have faith."

"Well what's the deal, then? Because it's getting ridiculous." Evidently Tucker's assumption that Dean's lying to me has really set me off. What's really bothering me might have nothing to do with Myra. It might just be my fear that Tucker's right about Dean.

"I can assure you that our officers are taking this issue very seriously—"

"I don't want the generic response. I need a real answer." He looks uncomfortable, so I add, "We're friends, right?"

He studies me for a moment and I try to soften my stare.

"This doesn't reach your friend Dean, got it?" he says.

"I won't tell him."

He eyes me up for a few more seconds and then says, "For several years now we've been working on getting our men inside the family's business to learn their secrets, but it's dangerous for the people going undercover and takes a long time to gain the family's trust."

So far none of this is news to me. Myra told me this back when I first learned about the Martellis.

"And then we have to wait for something to happen," he continues. "Luckily, Myra's case against Frank Lloyd helped us put away Michael Bello too. We'd known he was a high-ranking member of the Martelli crime family, but we hadn't been able to get him for anything substantial. That was, until his drug deal was discovered."

"Yeah, but a judge let him go," I add with a bit of resentment. I almost got shot that night I uncovered Bello's drug shipment coming in off a train. To think that Michael Bello is now free regardless of that, all because he was willing to break omertà, makes me angry.

"That wasn't our call, but it *did* provide us with crucial information, which we plan to use real soon."

"What do you mean?"

He shakes his head. "That's enough for now."

"Tucker, please. I need some glimmer of hope that there's still good in this city. That the Martellis are finally going to get what's coming to them."

He studies me for a long while. So long that I don't think he is actually going to tell me anything. Finally, he sighs and says, "We haven't moved in on any of Martelli's men because we had to verify the accuracy of his information with our informant. We couldn't risk sending our men into a trap."

"So who are you targeting?"

Tucker takes one final sip of his coffee, then gets up and reaches for his coat from the back of the chair. "I should get going."

"Not until you tell me who you guys are going after."

He laughs. "You're persistent. Just like your brother."

My face shows no sign of laughter while I wait for him to answer.

"Joe Gotti. Tonight, actually, which is why I need to get going."

"Are you planning it, then?"

"No, but they'll need extra manpower." He pulls on his coat. "You keep this all to yourself, understand?"

"I will."

"Good. I'm going to take off. Thanks for the coffee."

"Wait, I have another question. Do you think Bello is coming back to Olympia now that he's escaped custody?"

Besides the fact that I'm worried about Dean's continued involvement with his father, I'm also worried about what incriminating evidence the OPD has against him thanks to Bello's deal. Worse, what if Bello intends to kill everyone in the Martelli family? Regardless of status?

"I think that'd be very foolish of him, but we're not ruling it out. We have our feelers out in case he's spotted anywhere nearby. In the meantime, we need to keep moving on putting these guys away."

"Do you think a judge is going to let another one of them go?"

Chapter Eight

Tucker shrugs. "I really hope not, but I guess anything is possible. It's my job to gather evidence for an iron-clad case against them in order to make sure even a bribed judge can't let them go."

"Good." I slip my hands in my pockets to steady them. "So… can you tell me what you know about Dean?"

Tucker zips up his coat. "No."

"Can you at least tell me if you *do* have information on him?"

"We do."

More goose bumps as my heart pounds faster. "Okay."

He moves closer to the door and then turns back to me. "Look, Ethan, if he's really been staying away from his father like you said he's been, he has nothing to worry about."

I try to look relieved, but I know it's not good news. Dean could very well get himself in trouble by getting closer to his father. I need to convince him to back off. To forget his father for good. I thought I already had.

But should I just trust him? Dean looked me right in the eyes and told me I could. He hasn't let me down yet. When I go out as Fuse, he's always right beside me.

Without a mask.

Could he be arrested for working with Fuse? Would that make him a target based solely on the fact that the police would want to know more about Fuse?

It all makes me extremely uneasy. It's worsened by the fact that it seems like Dean's not taking my concerns seriously. About his involvement with his father or Fizz's identity. I guess the best thing I can do is trust him until he gives me a reason not to. I just hope I'm not signing my own death certificate by doing so.

———

JOE GOTTI'S ILLEGAL casino is on the Mid-Main Strip, which is a section along North and South Main Street outside of downtown where the streets merge back into one. The whole area is filled with a number of high-end retailers and is Olympia's most famous shopping district. It's similar to New York's

Fifth Avenue, Chicago's Millionaire Row, or Los Angeles's Rodeo Drive. Among the ritzy department stores, spas, and jewelers, it caters to the audience Gotti is after: rich people.

It wasn't hard to find the location. Well, at least it wasn't for me. Searching through the city's records of the area, I dug through until I found the right lease agreement under Gotti's name. The lease states the space is being used as a restaurant and banquet hall, although they haven't held a proper event in years and the menu is very limited. It's too simple, not only for the area but also for the aesthetic of the building.

The casino is actually a block away from North Main Street on Park Avenue, where some more retail shops have spilled over. The tree canopy and growing darkness obscures my view from my position on the rooftop of the Parkway Grill across the street from the casino, but I can see well enough to spot when something happens. Nothing yet.

Since it's Sunday, there aren't a ton of people out on the street, which is probably a good thing for the police raid. I don't know if I'll be needed here as Fuse, but I figured it couldn't hurt to come down here to make sure Gotti gets arrested.

Besides, it gets me out of the apartment so I don't have to talk to Dean. I know I need to at least consider his side, but I'm not there yet. Problem is, neither of us are wrong. He wants to protect his family as much as I want to protect mine.

No matter how Cale looks or what he's become, I can't justify turning on him. Whether I turn him in to the police or capture him somehow, it would send the message to Cale that I'm trying to hurt him, when instead I need to protect him. At least until I know for a fact that he's changed for the worse and is not just trying to get revenge for his attempted murder. If I were in his shoes, I'd be angry too. And maybe this is his way of trying to stop the redevelopment. Maybe if it's permanently shelved, he'll stop hurting people.

But I have to be honest with myself. He's not just hurting people, he's killing them. If I give him a pass at that, then that's condoning murder. Isn't that exactly what Dean's family does? Isn't that exactly the reason it's a bad idea for Dean to get involved with his family? I can't change my beliefs now. I'd only be moving the line because Cale's my brother.

I peer down at the street again and notice two police cars parked down the way a little bit. Lights off, but from what I can tell, both vehicles have people inside. Another minute later, two more police cars pull up on the street in the opposite direction. I notice Tucker sitting behind the wheel of one of them.

Guess the raid is about to start.

None of the policemen move toward the casino, but the atmosphere of the street turns tense as I notice the crowd has dispersed completely.

I spot three more police cars down a side street leading to North Main Street as Tucker and the rest of the policemen from the original four cars get out and begin moving in. They walk in the street, meaning they must've blocked them off.

Through the tree canopy, I try to get a good look at what's going on, but everything is still. A moment later, there's a soft *puff* as smoke billows out from the doors and windows. Policemen circle the area with weapons raised, preparing to catch anyone who runs out.

A few people pile out of the casino, running and coughing, but not as many as I'd expect. Still, they're caught by the waiting policemen.

Silence falls, and there's no more movement. I get an uneasy feeling, so I run to the back of the building and down the fire escape to the alley behind the line of officers.

Still no sign of anyone exiting the building. There have to be more people than that inside.

My eyes are glued to the entrance of the casino, which is visible between Tucker and another police officer. The cloud of smoke is still spewing out of the building. There's no way the men inside could stand the smoke bomb this long.

Unless they were prepared.

Gunshots fire out of the doorway of the building, and several officers fall to the ground, Tucker among them.

Sprinting out of my hiding place, I fire a streak of lightning toward the door to ward off the gunmen. I quickly pull Tucker behind a police car.

"You okay?" I try my best to disguise my voice.

He pats his chest and breathlessly says, "Kevlar."

I nod and run over to another policeman and help him over to Tucker. Before I have a chance to say anything to him, a bullet hits the windshield of the car we're hiding behind.

Peeking out around the car, I see a few of the men from the casino are coming out into the street. They're dressed in business suits with gas masks concealing their faces. No wonder they could hang out inside for that long.

One of them pops up from the front of the police car we're hiding behind and aims his gun at us. Before he has a chance to fire, I hit him square in the chest with my lightning. Dragging him behind the vehicle so I stay hidden, I pull his gas mask off.

"Cuff him and be prepared for more," I tell Tucker just before I pull the man's mask on myself.

Tucker doesn't have time to respond before I take off toward the entrance of the casino, zapping down anyone who decides to charge me. I keep it nonlethal. It's better if these men are arrested, not killed, in case they're willing to spill all like Bello was.

With the gas mask to protect me, I charge through the entrance of the casino. The smoke is thicker in here, and I can't see much.

Two hands grab me from behind, but I latch on to his arms and flip him over, sending a quick shock into his chest to keep him still. Two more men are inside the front entrance, and they don't see me until I'm right on top of them. I punch one in the face and clunk the second one's head against the wall. They both slump to the floor. I move outside long enough to wave some of the policemen in.

Back inside, I follow lights leading down a wide staircase that curves into a basement area. The smoke is thickest here, so I use the wall to guide myself around a corner. A black curtain hangs across the hallway, and the area behind it is mostly free of smoke. If Gotti's here, he won't be out in the open, especially not when the place is filled with smoke bombs.

There are several rooms off the hallway—two bathrooms, a kitchen—but the door at the end has a series of locks on it. My guess is that's where Gotti is.

I summon as much strength as I can and use both hands to zap the door. It blows in, and I feel a significant drain in energy. I suck in a deep breath and run quickly inside before whoever's on the other side of the door can get ahold of their gun.

There's a man trapped beneath the door and another one doing his best to block Joe Gotti's large body as he points his gun at me.

"Put the gun down," I tell him.

"Fuck off," the guard says.

As he raises it to fire at me, I use the last of my energy to zap him, throwing him back into Gotti. He slips to the floor unconscious.

"Come on," I tell Gotti. "It's over for you."

"Is it, Mr. Pierce?"

Luckily my face is hidden behind my Fuse mask and the gas mask so he can't see how stunned I am. I almost forgot he knows I'm Fuse. He was the one who drove me, Dean, and Carlo to the hospital that night Alexander attacked.

Gotti picks lint off his suit coat casually. "Interesting the way that things worked out. I really did think I was about to be arrested. I'm sure I will, but to my surprise, you're the one who showed up to apprehend me. What an interesting turn of events."

"Telling them who I am won't change anything."

"Oh, I have no intention of telling them you're Fuse. I'm sure the traitor Michael Bello has already told them as much. No, the part that I find interesting is that you're the one who is coming for me, which means that you're crossing Carlo Martelli. A fool's choice, I might add."

My mind races as I consider what Gotti's saying. How could I have a bigger target on my back from Martelli? Not to mention, how would Carlo even know I'm the one who found Gotti for the police?

None of that matters now. I'm here for Gotti, so that's what I'm going to do.

FUSE: OBLIVION

"I'd be willing to make a deal with you if—"

I shake my head. "No. No deal. You're going to jail." Swinging my fist, I get him right in the face. His large body slumps on top of his fallen guard and I step over the debris from the door to try to hoist him up.

Heavy footsteps down the hall tell me police are coming. With Gotti currently immobile, my work here is done. I pop open the small window Gotti would've never fit through and slip out into the alley.

Chapter Nine

I'm still not ready to talk to Dean yet, even though it's been a full twenty-four hours since our argument so I go right to the basement of the clinic after catching Joe Gotti. I know I won't have anything productive to say to Dean that won't result in another fight, so I'm just going to avoid him for now.

Besides, I'm still so hyped up from getting Gotti arrested that I know I couldn't sleep. Better to use my time wisely and figure things out. I decide to focus on what Michael Bello could be doing now that he's MIA. Meanwhile, I have the police scanners on in the background in case anything comes up that might be a sign of Cale.

So many things to juggle right now, but I need to do my best to keep the ball rolling for each of them.

The only new connection Bello has to Olympia that isn't speculation is the shootout that happened on Adams Street. That was Martelli's response to Bello for Luca's death, even though it was actually Fizz who killed him. But why would Martelli choose those men to go after?

It takes me a while, but I'm able to dig up traffic camera stills from that night of a group of men two streets over. Five of them, just as many who were there that night. It might not be them, but I decide to run their images through my facial recognition software anyway.

Each one has a driver's license that pops up when the search is complete. Only three of them have police records, though. One in particular, Miguel Wilson, has charges dating back to when he was thirteen. Drugs and assault, mostly. He spent five years in prison for one drug charge. He's the one who died during the shootout.

The other two, Kendrick Jackson and Treyvon Lawrence, don't have criminal careers as prolific as Wilson, but they're a far cry from innocent. Based on the hospital records I pull, they spent a few days at the First Olympian Medical Center downtown for treatment of the injuries they sustained during the shootout. From there, they were taken into police custody, but they were released on bail by a DeMarcus Paul.

I pull up the list of most dangerous gangs in the OPD's database and check the names against it. They're there. Even Paul. And if Martelli is targeting them, that means he thinks they're Bello's men. They must really be dangerous.

Would Bello come back to lead them against Martelli? Would the gang members even listen? What is Bello promising them to get them to cooperate?

Drugs and girls, probably. It makes me sick that that's their motivation, but Bello has the money and resources to provide that.

I let out another yawn and rub my eyes. It's almost midnight and nothing of significance has really shown up on the police scanner. Not anything that points to Cale, at least.

I'm tired and I know I'm going to dread getting up for work tomorrow. It's probably about time I head home and go to bed. Now that Dean's been using Cale's room, it's not like I have to worry about waking him up when I come in.

Just as I stand to gather my things to leave, a woman's voice comes over the police scanner.

"Just got a 9-1-1 about a shooting on Solar Drive. Possibly

that Fizz guy. Hinsley, can you check it out?"

"Sure thing, Jan," Hinsley replies.

Now that's something. Solar Drive is only a block away. It won't take me long to get there if I move quick.

Grabbing my Fuse mask, I race out the door into the cold night.

No sirens yet as I round the corner onto Solar. I stop dead in my tracks as soon as I get a clear view of the street, though.

Dark red drops of blood mar the dusting of snow. But if Cale attacked someone, the victim wouldn't be bleeding, they'd be melting. That means Cale must be the one who's hurt. Down the street, I hear the distinct roar of Fizz.

Cale.

I sprint toward the source of his cry, wondering how badly he's injured.

The street ends at Wyatt's rail yard, and through the chain-link fence I can see the giant mass of what Cale's become in the shadows. Three men surround him and throw rocks and other debris at him. One of them is very clearly Kendrick Jackson.

Although he spits acid at them, Jackson and his fellow thugs all jump out of the way to avoid getting hit.

I vault over the fence just as Jackson and another one of the men hook a cable around Fizz's sagging neck.

"Hey!" I bark as I run toward them. I can see a patch of blood on Cale's coat, and he falls to his knees as his thick fingers grasp at the cord around his neck.

"Not so tough now, huh?" Jackson taunts him.

One of the other two fires his gun at me, but I hold up my hand and hit him with lightning. He falls to the ground, shaking with electricity.

"Fuck, it's Fuse!" Jackson says. "Shoot the freak and let's get out of here!" He takes off in the opposite direction.

Before they have a chance to even aim, I'm on top of one of Jackson's lackeys and slam my fist into his face. I shove his arm to the ground and send electric charges through his body until his gun slips out of his hand.

Turning, I zap the other one just as he puts his gun against my head. He falls to the ground as well.

By time I get to my feet, Cale has already pulled off the cable and taken several careful steps away from me. He clutches his side and breathes heavily.

"Are you hurt?" I ask.

He steps backward, keeping his eyes on me.

"I'm not going to hurt you. I just want to make sure you're okay. I can help you."

My brother studies me, still unsure, still taking careful steps backward.

Stepping forward, I try a different approach. "Okay, we can just talk. Can you tell me how you got this way? Was it Martelli? Is that why you killed Leon Wallace?"

Everything comes out at once, even though I wish it hadn't. It sounds too much like an accusation.

He nods once.

The excitement of finally getting an answer to the question I've been searching for for months now gets the better of me, and I take several eager steps forward. Too much.

My brothers opens his mouth and roars, and I dive away onto the snow-covered pavement, but no acid spews from his mouth.

"Cale, it's—"

He's gone.

———

IRONICALLY, MONDAY MORNING is when I finally get a chance to breathe at work. After finishing up software development, checking panel installation, and attending the groundbreaking ceremony last week, I actually have very little to do this morning. I decide to check out the news to see if there's anything new about Fizz.

I wonder what he was doing in Hopman. That's a long way from the Works. Maybe he was looking for me—Fuse, rather—to help him take down the Martellis. But then, why would he run away when it was finally just the two of us? Maybe because he was bleeding and he wanted to get away from me in case I wasn't as friendly as he hoped. I don't know.

I just hope he's not hurt too bad. I didn't think his skin was penetrable, but apparently it only is by certain things. There's no telling how those chemicals altered his DNA. I've seen his body *absorb* bullets. But then, maybe he got caught on barbed wire or something. He's staying in multiple rooms at the Works, so he might be occupying other buildings throughout the city, meaning he's probably come across barbed wire often.

The biggest news story is still the attack at the ground-breaking ceremony and Leon Wallace's death. The police department put out a warning advising people to stay away from Fizz, which I can't really blame them for. At the end of the article, a note mentions that Fizz was recently spotted in Hopman, but that's it. There's also an article about Joe Gotti's arrest, but it doesn't tell me anything that I don't already know.

Myra's name catches my eye in one of the headlines: *"Did Connors collude with Fuse to get office?"*

When I click on the link to open it, I see it's an opinion piece by Lester Coltman. Of course. Despite the fact that it's an op-ed, it looks like it's just another news story. Coltman probably wrote it in response to Myra's comments about the mafia's influence in Hopman and the rest of the city. With the city leaders in a state of panic, everyone wants to find a scapegoat. Unfortunately, they keep pointing blame at Myra.

Right at the top of the article is the photo of Myra and Fuse outside city hall with the caption reading, *"Ms. Connors claims her encounter with Fuse was simply a warning for him to stay away."*

There are a lot of comments on the article, but after reading some nasty ones about Myra in the past, I vowed to myself to never read them when the article is about her. People are a lot braver when they're hidden behind their keyboards.

Ever since newly appointed councilwoman Myra Connors was spotted with Fuse, Olympia's "man in black" who himself has questionable motives, residents and officials have been questioning her credentials and capabilities.

Her first round of proposals for the troubled Hopman district that she represents received very lukewarm responses from fellow councilmembers, who asked for input from residents and a more comprehensive financial plan.

But with such limited credentials, how did Connors—who served as the assistant to former councilman Frank Lloyd for two years—get elected to a position on city council?

As is well-known, Connors was named an interim councilmember in the wake of Frank Lloyd's arrest last November and was elected the full position during a special election in December. Briefly, she had a competitor during the election when businessman James Alexander announced his intention to run. However, he mysteriously disappeared a week after announcing his candidacy and hasn't been seen since. Thus, his name never appeared on the ballot and Ms. Connors won the election.

The evidence presented right here in the Tribune *points to Ms. Connors working with Fuse in order to obtain her position on city council, likely on her path to becoming mayor. Her relationship with Fuse begs the question, Did she plant evidence against her predecessor, even going as far as to connect him to Michael Bello? The real estate developer has significant investments in the city. Upon their arrests, evidence suggested that they were both involved in the mafia and that Michael Bello was the mastermind behind their operation.*

Ms. Connors seems to be using Olympia's organized crime problem to hide her inadequacies for her new position. "[T]his city has a major issue with organized crime. With the poverty levels of my district, it's no wonder that Hopman is hit the hardest... [It'd] be interesting to see what would happen to the crime levels if the city was rid of this negative influence."

With the way Ms. Connors continues to point the

Chapter Nine

blame for her inexperience on other people, it's time to face the realization that maybe we as a city have failed to elect leaders who will live up to our expectations.

Chapter Ten

Myra's assistant said she wasn't in the office today when I called city hall at lunchtime. Despite my attempts to get her to tell me where Myra was, it wasn't until I called Myra's cell phone that I discovered she's working in Hopman today. Not in an office. Going door-to-door.

Naturally, I came down here immediately.

I walk down Lincoln Avenue, one of the oldest and most dense neighborhoods in the city. Most of the houses are small row houses that lead right into commercial buildings, so it's hard to tell where the residential street ends and where the commercial one begins. It's not hard to picture what this area looked like in its heyday. Seeing the mom-and-pop stores, restaurants, and other businesses boarded up adds to the depressing state of the neighborhood.

Many of the residents sit on their front steps since the buildings are so close to the street and don't have any front porches. A lot of the people are smoking, and some talk loudly to each other, but they all eye me suspiciously as I walk by. I don't fit into this neighborhood.

Chapter Ten

Neither does Myra, who's not hard to miss in her black skirt and matching jacket that fit snugly against her body. She's talking to a heavyset woman who's smoking on her front porch while two little girls ride their pink bikes up and down the sidewalk. They nearly run into me when I walk up.

"…make that happen. Believe me, I know it's tough." Myra holds her notepad against her chest as she talks to the woman, who raises her eyebrows at me as I approach. Myra follows her gaze and does a double-take when she sees me. "Oh, Ethan. I didn't think you'd come down here. Don't you have to work?"

"Lunch break. I don't have much time."

Myra turns and smiles at the woman and says, "Excuse me. It was nice talking to you, Shonda." She pats her notepad. "I've definitely made some notes about our discussion, and I'll be in touch."

The woman simply nods, and Myra leads us away.

We walk up the sidewalk a little farther before either of us say anything.

"What are you doing out here?" I ask.

"My job." I scrunch my eyebrows and she elaborates. "I'm tired of all the paper-pushing I do at city hall getting me nowhere. I was elected by these residents—even if I was the only one on the ballot—and I plan on doing right by them."

"Does this have anything to do with that article in the paper this morning?" As soon as I say it, I wish I hadn't. She told me she doesn't read the paper anymore. I should've remembered that.

"What article?" Her brow is furrowed as her eyes bore into mine.

"Never mind."

"I take it I got more bad press?"

I nod.

She puts a hand on her hip and lets out an exaggerated sigh. "What else is new? Yeah, I guess all the hate I've been getting lately is fueling this. The *Tribune* is not the only way to get my voice across to the people of this city. Coming down here and talking to the residents directly works too. Helps build a sense of trust, which is exactly what I need—what we *all* need in this city. I have to show them that I'm here for them. That I want to work to better their lives because I know what it's like out here."

I look up and down the street and notice a number of eyes on us. "But Myra, I'm not sure it's a good idea for you to be out here by yourself. This is dangerous."

"It's only dangerous for a white boy like you." She smiles quickly before continuing. "But seriously, I grew up in Hopman. I've been working on this district for two years. I know what parts to avoid. Actually, when I tell people stories about where I grew up, their whole attitude changes. They like me more because I'm from here. Because I'm me. Because I'm not trying to be anything different. I'm real with them. There are obviously still people who don't want to have anything to do with me, but this door-to-door thing seems to be working for the most part."

This idea still puts me on edge, but I decide to humor her for a bit. "What are you even talking to them about?"

"My proposals and ideas. The rest of the council said I needed resident support, so I'm getting it. A lot of these people seem pretty hopeful after we get done talking. Most of them don't even know they have a new councilwoman."

"Well, it's good that they seem to be liking what you're saying. Still, why didn't you bring someone else from your office? So you're not out here alone."

"Ethan, I'll be fine."

"But it'd make me feel better—"

"Just stop!" Her voice carries down the street, and she immediately lowers it. "Look, with Cale missing and everything that people are saying about me, I just feel like I need to do *something*. I can't sit in that office at city hall for another day without getting back in touch with reality." She motions around. "*This* is reality. *This* is what I'm working for. *This* is why I'm employed. I can't forget that. Otherwise, I'll become just like the person I replaced."

I smile because I'm proud of her. She never stands down from what she believes in, and even though it's an uphill battle, she's going to fight it. Besides, it's not like there's even a chance that she's going to listen to me anyway.

And I can relate. More than once I've reached the point of desperation. The urge to do something when the world seemed to be crumbling. It's how I became Fuse. By doing something reckless. By doing something crazy. By doing *something*. I can't tell Myra not to when I've done the same thing.

"Just…be careful, okay? Call me if anything happens or if you need a ride. I'll come. No matter what."

She smiles and hugs me. "Thanks, Ethan."

"And don't stay out after dark," I add.

Laughing, she says, "I won't."

I walk back to Canal Street to the subway. My mind does somersaults. Myra is just trying to do her job, and the *Tribune* and its so-called reporters are tearing her down because of it. I can't help but think that this is all a master plan of Carlo Martelli's. That he's igniting a smear campaign against Myra to get the attention off of the mob war. Either that or he doesn't like it that Myra's someone on the council that he can't control. She's already lost all the people who are important to her. The only thing left is her job.

My phone buzzes in my pocket, and when I pull it out I see it's Dean. Great.

"So when are we going to do something about your father?" Not the best way to start a conversation, but it certainly sets the mood.

"What?" Dean asks, confused. "Ethan, I just had lunch with him. What do you think he's done now?"

I tell him about Myra. About the article in this morning's paper. Remind him of the other things that have been said about her. Tell him about Cale and what Carlo did to him.

"Oh, the mutant told you, did he?" Dean cuts in.

"It's Cale, Dean. I think that much is obvious by now."

"Why? Because of a T-shirt that could be anybody's and a few newspaper clippings?"

"You didn't see the room, okay? He's following Myra through the press, which, thanks to your father, is only bad press lately."

"That's not necessarily my father's doing. Now that Bello's

out, it could be him. It could be a disgruntled coworker. It could just be an asshole reporter. Maybe he's an ex-boyfriend of hers or something."

"Sounds to me like you're fishing for excuses to protect Carlo."

"And it sounds to me like you're looking for reasons to go after him."

"And why shouldn't I?"

"Ethan, I'm sorry this is happening to Myra," he says. "It sucks. She's a good person and I want to see her succeed, but you're way off base here. This attack against her reputation isn't fueled by my father. Killing him won't stop the things they're saying about her. She's a public figure. It's going to happen."

He sounds sincere, but I still want to protect her. Besides, I really hate it that he so easily shot down every one of my arguments. And that he's so protective of Carlo. Why is Dean getting closer to him again? Shouldn't he of all people realize how dangerous Carlo is? It doesn't matter that he saved Dean and me. He took Cale's life and so many others. He needs to be brought down.

———

THE STREETS OF Little Italy are pretty empty tonight. I take advantage of it to sneak into the alley that leads to the Little Italy Food Company. But first I tuck into the darkest corner of the alley and dig through my bag for my Fuse suit.

These arguments I've been having with Dean about his relationship with his father are never going to go away. I don't want to lose Dean, but the way he's allowing himself to be sucked into his father's grasp scares me. First the favors, now lunch. I thought we were in agreement that Carlo is not someone we want to be associated with. Guess not.

That's why I want to have a conversation with Carlo. See if I can figure out what his plans are for Dean. We had a civil conversation before, after Dean was hurt by Alexander. Maybe this time will be similar. The suit is just added protection for me in case anyone else sees me or if things turn ugly. Probably wasn't the smartest idea that I didn't tell anyone I was coming out here, but I've been in more dangerous situations than this before.

Once my suit is on, I hide my bag behind a dumpster and continue down the alley toward the restaurant.

The last time I was at the Little Italy Food Company, Dean had to save me from being killed by Michael Bello and his men. But I don't need Dean tonight.

There's a guard dressed in all black by the backdoor of the restaurant. He's stocky and standing attentive as he keeps an eye out for trouble, but he still doesn't spot me in the shadows of the alley. As I creep closer to him, I shoot a streak of lightning at the dumpster in the corner. When he goes to check it out, I move in from behind him.

Using the lessons I learned from Dean, I shove his gun hand up in the air as he fires once. With his arm in my grasp, I shuffle in front of him and vault him over my back until he's lying flat on the ground. With ragged breaths—he was heavier than I thought—I kick the gun out of his reach.

Leaning over, I mutter in a deep voice, "Go in and get your boss so we can have a chat."

The guard chuckles through heavy breaths. "Funny, kid."

He tries to get up but I push him back down. Letting the energy course through my body, I release just the slightest trickle of electricity. Enough to warn him that I can do much worse.

"Just him," I say. "No one else. Just to chat."

Offering my hand, I help him up after he nods. I creep back to the shadows as I wait for Carlo to emerge, making sure I have a solid escape plan in case more guards show up and start shooting at me.

A few minutes later, Carlo comes out in a black suit with a red pocket square. His guard follows closely behind.

"I suppose there's a reason Olympia's man in black is usually only seen at night," Carlo says, looking around slowly. He has a smirk on his face.

"Show your fucking face, coward," the guard bellows behind him.

"It's okay, Peter," Carlo tells him. "Fuse is just waiting for you to leave. But if he thinks I'm going to talk to him in a dark alley alone, then he's mistaken. Especially since I'm sure he's well aware of the state of business lately." He turns back to the fence, still looking for me. "So, Fuse, I'll send my man inside if you come out with your mask off."

Seems like a trap. If he knows I'm Fuse, what difference does it make if my mask is off? But I don't want to waste any more time.

Slowly, I step into the light and Carlo turns to face me.

"Ah, there you are. Now, the mask?"

I shake my head and deepen my voice. "He leaves."

"Oooh, that was scary," Carlo teases with a grin. He studies me, expecting me to back down and give in to his demands, but I don't. "Very well. Peter, you may go."

The guard seems to hesitate but relents and returns inside.

"The mask?"

I ignore his comment and lock eyes with him as I consider the best way to start.

He doesn't let the silence last and says, "Well, if you came to me dressed up as Fuse, I'm assuming you want something. So tell me, what is it you're after? Money? Everyone wants money. Fame? I have a few contacts who could build up your reputation. My son? Well…" He chuckles.

"What are your intentions with Dean?"

"Ah, so it is my son." He slips his hands in his pockets.

"Why are you suddenly asking favors of him, calling him, going to lunch with him?"

"I didn't know it was a crime for a father to spend time with his son."

"So that's it? You're not trying to recruit him?" I have to at least consider the possibility that I'm reading into this. Still, I'm not completely convinced.

"We're family, and what's more important than that?" he asks with a smirk.

I stare at him. Carlo's word is about as trustworthy as that pit of chemicals he threw Cale into.

"Of course, family *does* help each other out from time to time."

"So you *are* trying to recruit him back to the mob, aren't you?"

He makes a face. "This is not some fraternity, Mr. Pierce. This is business."

I nod slowly as it all becomes clear. "Oh, I see how it is. You're only interested in having a relationship with Dean so that you can use his relationship with me to get to Fuse."

Carlo watches me with a grin.

"But Dean wants more than that. He wants a real father-son relationship. So much so that he's blind to what's really going on."

"And what do you think *is* going on?"

"I think you need Dean to go through the motions of joining the business like everyone else because the rest of the family didn't like his sudden return at Thanksgiving. If you're going to keep Dean happy, you need to be able to bring him around for holidays. And the only way you can do that while maintaining your status as the boss is if the rest of the family thinks Dean earned his place back. All to get to me."

He waves a finger at me. "You are certainly more than you appear, Mr. Pierce. But I believe you have an inflated ego if you believe all of this is because of you. Only a few of your loved ones who have gotten in the way of my plan, but you can't just move on. No, because you're Fuse. You see, it's more of a nuisance than anything."

He's talking about Cale and Myra.

I charge him, shoving him against the brick wall, my forearm pressed against his chest. I want to get the confession out of him that he threw Cale in the chemical pit, but I can't let him know that I know. Then he would be targeting Fizz even more. He probably doesn't realize Cale is Fizz.

Instead, I turn to the only other person I can protect right now.

"You tell your buddies at the *Tribune* to lay off Myra Connors. She has done nothing to you!"

Carlo smiles. "My contacts at the *Tribune* are their own

people. The only favors I call in to them are to suggest stories they should avoid. I'm not paying them to write. That's not what I do."

I press my arm into him more. "You know *exactly* what you're doing, and you can make it stop. Tell them to back off."

"Or what? You'll kill me? I think you and I both know that someone else will take my place at the top if I'm gone. If a Martelli is lucky enough to take the helm, I daresay it might even be your beloved Dino."

Could Dean really take over for Carlo? Is that what his goal is for him? Would the rest of the family let him? More importantly, would Dean do it? There'd be no saving him then. Of course, Carlo could just be saying that to get to me.

Swinging my free arm, I punch Carlo right in the gut and step back as he bends over to clutch at his stomach.

When he stands up straight again, his breathing still heavy, he flashes me a smile. "I'd be careful who you upset in this city. Wouldn't want anything else to happen to you and your friends now, would we, Ethan?"

———

I'M STILL LIVID by time I get back home. Talking to Carlo only proved that he's leading Dean down a dark road. At this point, we've argued about it and I've expressed my concerns about Carlo so much that he's not even going to believe me that his father is just using him.

"Where have you been?" Dean peeks his head out of the bathroom with a toothbrush hanging out of his mouth.

"Out." I throw my bag in my room and pour myself a glass of water. I know I should tell him what I learned, even if he doesn't believe me, but I don't want to get into it right now. I feel like a failure.

He spits and rinses off the brush. "Fuse?"

"Yeah."

"Did you get 'em?"

"I don't want to talk about it."

"'Kay," Dean says before he shuts the door to his bedroom loudly behind him.

Yeah, he's still pissed. I guess I can't blame him for the way I yelled at him on the phone earlier. Maybe asking me about my night and initiating conversation was his way of extending the olive branch.

Unless he knows that I talked to Carlo tonight and totally betrayed his trust. I'm sure Carlo already called him to tell him all about it.

I groan. I can't get out of my own head. Even though last night was a late night and today was a long day, I don't feel tired as I get ready for bed. I decide it'd be no use trying to sleep just yet.

Sitting against the headboard of my bed, I text Myra, even though it's almost eleven.

How'd it go in Hopman today?

A few minutes later, she replies, *Good, thanks for asking.*

I want to ask her more about it. What she learned, who she talked to, if she genuinely felt safe going door to door, but I can't think of the best way to put it into words—especially in a text—so I let it go. I'll call her later.

Hopefully I didn't mess things up for her by talking to Carlo. I was stupid to establish the connection between me and Myra. Now he knows she's one of my weak spots. But he's also not ignorant to the fact that Dean's another weak spot for me. The mob boss seems to be the root of a bunch of the problems in my life. Not only as Fuse, but personally too. I wonder how things would be between me and Dean if his father wasn't who he is.

Dean made it clear the other day that he wants to be with me but he's not ready yet. And I want to be with him, but do I honestly think I'm ready? By himself, Dean is great. But people never come by themselves. They come with baggage. All of their other connections that make them whole. Am I ready to be with him completely, crooked bloodline and all? The resentment I've been feeling toward him because of his family says otherwise.

I *do* care for him and I *do* want to be with him. I just wish this whole business with Carlo would go away.

Chapter Eleven

The next morning, I'm sitting at the counter eating a bowl of cereal when Dean exits the bathroom wearing just a towel and goes straight to Cale's room. Without a word to me, either. I'm not sure how to take that.

A part of me wishes I hadn't given him Cale's room. Cale's not dead. But at the same time, he's never going to be the same. He probably won't ever use the room again. What's the standard for keeping someone's belongings intact to honor their memory sufficiently before going through it all and moving on? Especially when they're not technically dead. I still haven't had the heart to tell Myra that I've already rented out his room. I know she'd understand, but it doesn't mean it'll hurt any less.

Dean comes out dressed in a red polo and black windbreaker pants and pours himself a glass of water.

"Been to the gym already?" I ask.

"Yeah." He stuffs a water bottle in his bag. "Sorry I didn't wait for you. I wasn't sure where your head was at."

You and me both, dude, I think. But I just nod and say, "Right. Sorry for being grumpy last night. It's just everything, you know?"

Chapter Eleven

"Sure, yeah." He pauses and looks at me as if he's considering saying something.

"What?" I ask.

"Nothing, never mind." He turns to the door.

"Dean, wait." This has been bothering me all night. "I need to tell you about what I was doing last night, and I'm sure you'll be mad, but I just have to be honest."

"You went and talked to my father." He keeps his eyes on the countertop.

"Did he tell you?"

He nods. "Called just before you came home."

"Dean, I'm sorry. I should've just come to you, but I'm worried. You're doing favors for him, you're having lunch with him, he's calling you as soon as I talk to him. It just seems off."

He rolls his eyes and turns away.

"Are we even going to talk about this?"

"Why should we? Because you can't even take my word for it that I'm not rejoining the family? Ethan, I know where the line is. I haven't crossed it yet. So just do me a favor and butt out." He slings his bag over his shoulder and leaves.

When he's gone I'm left wondering if things will ever truly be okay between us.

———

I'VE BEEN HUNCHED over my computer all morning focused on the diagnostic reports for the installed solar roadway panels. Despite being inspected upon installation, there are still issues that pop up when we try to access each one remotely. That tells me there's a problem with the code, meaning we can fix it in the office. Only trouble is, we have to find the error in a sea of gibberish. Needless to say, I'm tired.

I stopped volunteering to go out in the field now that JD is more than capable of handling it on his own. Not to mention, my work back in the office kept piling up.

After checking off a number of things on my to-do list this morning, I decide to go down to the break room to enjoy my lunch. Usually I sit at my desk and read the news or do some research for Fuse stuff, but I deserve a break after the morning I've had. A moment to just unwind and forget about everything—work, Fuse, Dean, Cale, Myra. All of it.

I settle in at a table in the corner and pull up an e-book on my phone. My eyes scan over the virtual pages as I open the plastic grocery bag, pull out my turkey sandwich, and begin to chow down. It's delicious. I picked it up on my way in since I cut my workout short in Dean's absence.

Just a long run today. I'll have to do weights tomorrow to keep my strength up. Ideally, I'd like to do combat training again, but with the way things have been up and down between me and Dean lately, who knows whether we'll be at each other's throats or best friends come tomorrow morning.

"…owned by Michael Bello," I overhear one of the guys at the table next to me whisper to his friends. I don't recognize him from my department. Three of them are seated at the table, and although they're talking quietly amongst themselves, their voices carry in the small break room. At first, it was difficult to concentrate on my book, but the mention of Bello steals away any idea of reading.

"Well, used to be," he continues. "I don't know what the hell's going on with it now. Beautiful place, though."

"Yeah, amazing how that whole neighborhood has changed," another one says. He's a scrawny guy who looks like he's swimming in his blue dress shirt.

"Bello did most of that neighborhood," the first one adds. He's huskier with a patch of hair on his chin.

"I was surprised. He seemed like a stand-up guy, and now he's supposedly connected to the mafia? Not to mention the guy who's running around spitting acid in people's faces." The third guy shakes his head. He's wearing a brown sweater with the sleeves pushed up. "First Fuse, now this guy. How many more freaks can this city take on?"

"You think Fuse is just as bad as Fizz?" Blue Shirt asks quietly. "Fuse hasn't killed anyone, has he?"

"Don't be so sure with the way things are in Hopman,"

Husky says. "We don't know if Fuse has had to kill in order to calm down some of those gangs he goes after. That whole district has gone to shit. I say we should just bulldoze the whole thing."

"And what about the Works?" Blue Shirt asks. "Isn't that what they're trying to do?"

"Yeah, until that Fizz guy showed up. Call in a firing squad," Brown Sweater murmurs, trying to keep his voice down. We're the only four in the break room right now.

Husky chuckles. "Or send Fuse after him!"

Brown Sweater shakes his head. "This city is crazy."

Silences falls between them for a moment and I try to return to my book. Sometimes it's easy to forget that normal, everyday people that I work with know about some of the stuff related to Fizz. And they're all interpreting it differently than I am.

"I wonder if Bello and Rizzoli are still close," Husky whispers.

My ears perk up.

Brown Sweater scrunches his brow. "What do you mean?"

"When I first started—what was it? Maybe ten years or so ago?—Rizzoli's office had a few pictures of him on vacations with Bello, along with their wives." Husky elbows Blue Shirt and chuckles. "I don't think Rizzoli's ex took his friendship with Bello in the divorce."

It makes sense. For Rizzoli and Bello to both have the positions they did in Martelli's camp—even if Bello is no longer playing nice—they must've been working together with Carlo for a long time. Must've spent a lot of time together. And if they vacationed together on top of that, that means they had a friendship outside of their work with Martelli's business.

Bello and his wife's presence at that dinner party Rizzoli invited me to back in October seems obvious now. They were genuine friends who invited the potential threat over to schmooze him. I was the odd man out at that party. Even Leon Wallace must've known it was a ruse to feel me out.

Bello was probably getting frustrated that he was a capo in the worst district of the city. He probably wanted more power, which would explain why he purchased property in other parts of the city. And Rizzoli, being Carlo's right-hand man, would've been the perfect person to chummy up to for a better district.

I can't resist scooting my chair over and butting in to their conversation. "Sorry for interrupting, but I didn't know Rizzoli and Bello were such good friends. I knew they knew each other, but I didn't realize they were so close."

Blue Shirt and Brown Sweater shoot me a worried look, but Husky ignores them and nods. "Oh yeah. Inseparable for a long while. Bello was here so much that for the first few years I worked here, I thought he did too."

"So why do you think he escaped police custody?" Blue Shirt asks.

"Probably to recruit his buddy Rizzoli to overthrow the mafia," Brown Sweater mutters.

"Why do you say that?" I ask.

"Well, they've worked together before, haven't they?" Husky says. "Robert Moyer, for instance."

I look between the three of them, confused.

Husky starts, "Robert Moyer died suddenly—"

"Killed, if you ask me," Brown Sweater interrupts.

"And then Frank Rizzoli became CEO," Husky continues.

"So you think Bello and Rizzoli killed Moyer?" I ask. "But what would Bello get out of that?"

Husky sits back and puts up his hands. "I don't know. All I'm saying is that Rizzoli has connections to the mafia. He was real good friends with Bello and then hired Joe Gotti to be his assistant."

Finally, I make the connection. "And Gotti just got arrested for operating an illegal casino."

"And there are rumors that he's also involved in the mafia," Husky says. "But we should be careful about talking about this here. I don't think it's a far stretch to say Rizzoli is too."

———

Chapter Eleven

"NO, I DIDN'T get murdered," Myra chuckles into the phone. "But I appreciate your concern, Ethan."

The first thing I did when I got home was call Myra to see how her trip to Hopman went yesterday. I wanted to elaborate on our short text exchange from last night.

"How'd it go?" I ask as I take a seat on the couch in the living room. Dean's not home yet, so I have the place to myself.

"Well, better than I thought it would," she starts. "It's going to take a lot of work, but the fact that someone from city council was even showing an interest in the residents of Hopman made a huge difference in their perception. They're still skeptical, but I have hope."

"That's good."

I felt kind of guilty about not calling her last night, but hearing the optimism in her voice makes me feel better. She sounds different. Happier. More alive than she's sounded in months.

"What do you have in mind to change the neighborhood?"

"Well, the development proposals I've seen want to tear a lot of it down to build slum apartments, basically."

Reminds me of what I overheard at work. "People still do that?"

"Yeah. The same thing is happening at the Works, they're just calling it 'low-income housing.' Basically, it's a way to shove off the poor people to a designated area of the city to keep them away from the rest of society and trap them in the perpetual cycle of poverty. People of color, mostly."

"Oh wow. I guess I never thought of it that way," I admit.

"Yeah. So the fact that I was interested in preserving the neighborhood and rebuilding a true sense of community, as opposed to something that will make a rich man a quick profit, was a real selling point for them."

"I'm glad that they listened to you. Now if you can just avoid the bad press long enough to get something done."

She huffs a short laugh. "Yeah. My colleagues haven't exactly been the most receptive of me, either, but they don't have to like me for me to make a difference. It'll take a little extra work on my part, but if I can power through it, I should be able to rally

"

together some of these residents to do something. I just have to be careful not to do anything that would let them down. Or appear that way. They've been lied to and played so much that they're not very trusting of people like me."

"With good reason, though."

"Absolutely. I just hope the *Tribune* doesn't get wind of me going door to door until I've built up the residents' confidence in me a bit more. Developed a relationship, you know? It's going to take time."

The door opens behind me and I turn to see Dean walk through. He offers a tight smile and kicks off his shoes.

"Sounds like you need to get to work. Call me if you need anything," I say just before we hang up.

"Who was that?" Dean riffles in the fridge and pulls out a package of meat he must've thawed this morning.

"Myra. She seems to have made some headway with the people who live in Hopman."

"That's good." He moves to the stove.

I sigh and force myself to swallow my pride enough to take the high road and start a conversation so we can move past this disagreement. It seems so simple, but it takes a lot to voice it. "Dean, I'm sor—"

"Have you killed Fizz yet?" He says over me.

Narrowing my eyes, I stare at his back since he refuses to look at me. "What? No, I haven't."

"Because you think he's your brother," he says.

"I know he is."

He turns around. "Even if he is, he's sure as hell not the same person."

"Doesn't mean I should kill him," I say with attitude. Then, "Your father didn't."

He slaps a spatula against the countertop and the smack makes me jump. "That's enough of that!"

"No, Dean. I don't know if you just think I'm trying to control you or something, but your father is dangerous. But you're too busy doing favors for him to see it!"

"What makes you think I'm still doing favors for him?"

"Well, have you stopped?"

He turns away.

"Exactly my point."

He rubs his forehead and softens his stance. "Let's just forget about that. We shouldn't be fighting. We make a good team, and that's exactly what we need to be right now. A team."

"Dean—"

"You're right." He cuts me off. "My father is dangerous. But—"

"But nothing," I say. "I don't want to fight with you either, but I'm worried you're going to end up dead from getting too close to him. Look at the pain he's already brought you."

He turns back to the stove. "My father won't be a problem for much longer."

"Why's that?"

"He's in a transitional phase of his life."

"Transitional how? Like he's retiring?"

Dean shrugs.

That would be another reason Carlo is trying to bring Dean back into the family.

"So why doesn't he just talk to Bello and figure out a compromise?" I ask. "Bello's out, isn't he? I'm sure your father could put out the word that he wants to talk to him to come to a truce."

He gives me a look. "My father doesn't compromise."

"Well, he needs to do something. I'm sure Rizzoli would be able to figure something out with how close he is with Bello."

Dean turns and looks at me with confusion. "What are you talking about?"

"A few guys at work said that Bello and Rizzoli are really close. Or they were, rather."

"Close how?"

I roll my eyes. "Not like you and I have been close, but they're good friends."

Dean's cheeks darken a bit. "Oh. So what?"

"So it got me thinking that if Bello is trying to overthrow Martelli, who would Rizzoli's loyalty be with?"

"My father, hands down."

"Are you sure? You just said it yourself, your father is getting older. And even when he was in police custody, Bello still found a way to maintain power in Olympia."

Dean waves it off and returns to the sizzling meat on the stove. "My father's been through other things like this. He'll get through it."

"Then tell me, how did James Alexander get to the roof of Tranidek Tower when the roof entrance is off of Rizzoli's floor? And why did Rizzoli sneak out early from Thanksgiving dinner without a word to anyone? You ever think that maybe he's the one who helped put that corpse on your bike with Alexander? James must've been in talks with Michael Bello, who had already recruited Frank Rizzoli, so when it came time for Alexander to put that body on your bike, Rizzoli was his lookout."

I try to read Dean's expression from his back. He doesn't say anything. Doesn't move. Just stares down at the pan on the stove. For a minute, I consider whether he heard me, but he's only standing a few feet away.

"Dean, I think Rizzoli is helping Bello overthrow your father."

CHAPTER TWELVE

Fuse: Savior or Sociopath?
By: Lester Coltman

Fuse, Olympia's "man in black"—often awarded the title of the city's hero, thanks to his lifesaving tendencies—may not be such a saint after all. A never-before-seen photo submitted by a faithful Tribune *reader yesterday shows the masked man fleeing the Hopman neighborhood on the back of a Ducati motorcycle during the shootout last Saturday.*

"I'm not denying the number of arrests he's assisted," Mayor Eugene Banks said during a phone interview. "Officials down at the Olympia Police Department credit him with numerous arrests in the last five to six months. However, he tends to instill a sense of chaos wherever he goes. Chaos does not equate to a safe, friendly city."

While no official warrant is out for Fuse's arrest, Police Detective Tucker Cross says he is definitely a person of interest in a number of crimes.

Fuse: Oblivion

"He's saving people…[but he should] leave the crime fighting to the professionals," Cross said.

This photo comes after reports that Councilwoman Myra Connors worked with Fuse in order to plant evidence against former Councilman Frank Lloyd in an effort to get herself elected into his position, a scheme that seemed to work in her favor. Connors had not returned any calls to her office by press time.

My blood is boiling by time I finish reading. I knew it was only a matter of time before Fuse became another scapegoat for the city's problems, but I thought they'd forget about Myra in the process. That unnecessary little reminder at the end of the article may have cost Myra the progress she made with the residents of Hopman. That is, if they even read the paper.

What originally caught my attention to the article wasn't Fuse's name at the forefront of the article, but the picture of Dean's bike. He's always careful to remove his license plates before coming out with me as Fuse, but what if they identify him another way? I can't stand the thought of bringing both him and Myra down because of me. Not when I'm protected by a mask.

Besides, I expected Dean's father to be the one to get him in trouble again, not me. Good thing Dean was wearing his helmet in the photo. It's about the closest thing he has to a mask.

Clicking through to another page, I see another article about me. Well, Fuse. It's another opinion piece. Luckily, there's no accompanying picture to draw people's attention. Still, that doesn't mean it won't be read—and believed—by some people.

Fuse: What does he want?
By: Natalie Caulkins

By now, most Olympians are aware of the "man in black" lurking the streets at night in a costume fit for Halloween. Although the season has ended, this masked vigilante remains. His actions leave many residents wondering—and fearing—what does he want?

Chapter Twelve

Looking back, the man known as "Fuse" has been spotted in the middle of drug deals and shootouts, and at the scene of the first victim of a bizarre and horrific murder downtown last November. This was also around the time he was first spotted with Councilwoman Myra Connors.

Despite hopes that Fuse is the city's saving grace when it comes to its rising violent crime rate, it seems as though, looking at his history, Fuse is not our protector. In fact, he may even be the one causing the crime rates to increase.

According to—

I stop reading because I can't take any more bad news. Not when the *Tribune's* writers seem to be *looking* for things to exploit.

Despite what the paper says, I know I'm making a difference as Fuse. The number of violent crimes is up because of the mob war between Martelli and Bello. And Fizz's recent murders haven't helped, either. It has nothing to do with me as Fuse.

But the articles still put me in a bad mood the rest of the day. Even as I head out to the sidewalk to go home after work, my mind runs wild. Should I just quit being Fuse? Let the number of violent crimes rise even higher? Stand by as innocent people are taken advantage of? Murdered? Abused? Will it even matter? Will the *Olympia Tribune* ever run a retraction to the lies they've been spewing about me? Is my mask to blame for garnering harsh criticism? Would people miss me if I was gone?

Of course they would. I have to believe that. When all else seems to be failing, the best I can do is keep going. I *know* I've saved people's lives. The girls in Bello's prostitution ring. The innocent citizens of Hopman who would be victimized by crime. Not to mention the policemen who raided Gotti's casino.

Rationally, it all makes sense—and I know I should just ignore the *Tribune*—but I still can't get my mind off the idea that I'm useless.

I'm still fuming by time I reach my apartment building. It's cold and I can see my breath in the streetlights. I'm so focused on getting inside that I don't notice the black sedan sitting on the side of the street until the window rolls down.

"Mr. Pierce," Carlo's voice calls from the back seat.

I look up and down the street. The walkers don't seem to take notice of the strange car. Reluctant and fearful, I step forward. I'm surprised he came here alone to kill me. After all, I manhandled him the other day, and I know a man like Carlo Martelli won't let that go unnoticed.

The driver—someone new now that Joe Gotti is in jail—opens the door for me and I slide in. Quiet envelops us once the door shuts. The windows are tinted so not much of the streetlight glow reaches inside. I consider being the first to say something, but I don't know what I'd say. I shouldn't have gotten in the car.

"I trusted you, Mr. Pierce," Carlo starts.

With the *Tribune* articles still on my mind, I ask, "With what?"

"I invited you to share a holiday with me and my family. Allowed you to continue your relationship with my son. Trusted you with some of my secrets."

I want to correct him about me and Dean, but I know interrupting him won't help matters at all.

"I even kept *your* secret, Mr. Pierce." He shakes his head. "And I've forgiven you for the way you assaulted me the other day."

He's looking out the front window so I feel safe rolling my eyes.

"And you couldn't even come to me like a man," he goes on.

"Come to you about what?"

"Had to read about it in the paper." He wags a finger at me. "I don't like to be surprised like that, Mr. Pierce. I take great offense to that kind of behavior."

Forcing politeness, I say, "I'm sorry, *sir*, but I have no idea what you're talking about."

"I'm talking about you assisting Michael Bello. The very man we discussed after Thanksgiving. The one you've been blaming for young Emma Landry's death."

My body tenses up as her name rolls off his tongue.

"You knew he was no longer an ally of this family, but evidently loyalty means nothing to you as you kept this piece of information to yourself."

"I'm not working with Michael Bello." Frank Rizzoli's name is on the tip of my tongue, but I hold it back.

"You used your power as Fuse to support the gangs in Mr. Bello's faction against me."

"What!" I exclaim. "Why would I support the gangs?"

"And then you assisted the men in blue in arresting one of my men."

He must've finally heard I helped with the raid on Joe Gotti. Or just decided to finally act on it.

"Power is a tricky thing, boy," he continues. "Once a man has a taste of it, he tends to get greedy. Now it's public knowledge that you were in Hopman the night the Adams Street gang attacked my men. And I have it under good authority that Fuse struck one of my men with his supernatural ability."

"I didn't hit him," I interrupt. I made sure to hit the street, not anyone in particular.

Carlo smirks. "That's not what I heard from men who are more trustworthy than yourself. And since you've chosen to come after me through my men, it's a shame to say, but you will never be forgiven. No matter what your relationship is with my son, some things aren't meant to be broken."

"You're talking about omertà, but I didn't break it." Technically, I haven't told anyone anything about Martelli's business. "And speaking of betrayal, what about what you did to my brother?"

"Cale Pierce needed to be stopped!"

"And you couldn't have given him more warnings to stop?"

"*More* warnings? Mr. Pierce, I do not give out warnings."

Interesting. So the Black Hand Letter wasn't from him. But then, who sent it?

"An associate of mine came to me for help in keeping your brother was silenced once and for all."

Leon Wallace.

"The fact that he met his demise at the Works was fitting,

don't you think?" he continues.

"No, I don't think it's fitting," I say. "Cale was just trying to help people with his story."

"Like you attempt to do as this Fuse person?"

"Yes."

"Well, I have to say, your actions contradict that statement. In fact, I think it would be wise of you to stop being Fuse. A man shouldn't have to hide behind a mask. True bravery is being able to face the world without any protection. Just as your friend Miss Connors is doing."

His words have a bigger impact on me than I realized anything he could say would. Am I really just using Fuse as a way to hide from the world? Would I be able to continue to do what I do without the mask? Would I want to?

One thing that isn't going to happen, though, is that I'm not going to stop doing this. Going out as Fuse—with or without the suit—helps people. It saves people. It gives them hope. Not only that, but it gives me something to fight for. Something to work toward. Something to be proud of. Fuse is a part of who I am. It's helped me work through a lot over these last six months. I'm not willing to let that go. Especially not at Carlo's demand.

"No," I shake my head. "You're wrong." Bold words, but I press on. "I might've helped the police with Gotti, but I'm not helping Bello. I'm not helping you anymore, either. The only people that I'm helping are the Olympians who want to make this city a better place. People who need someone to look up to. I'm not playing any more of your games."

He takes a deep breath and fixes the cuffs of his suit. "Very well."

I reach for the door handle, but he speaks up again.

"However, that does leave me with few options."

I stop and glare at him.

"If you refuse to end your charade as Fuse, I'll have to either find a way to permanently kill your brother or tell the world who you are myself. I'm feeling rather generous, so I'll let you pick."

My blood turns cold. How did he find out Cale is Fizz? Probably just assumed, I guess. Does he know where Cale's living now? Will Cale be able to protect himself?

As for my identity, I know Carlo would do it. He wouldn't even lose sleep over it. He doesn't care. All he cares about is bettering himself. Making more money. Taking more control. He doesn't care how many lives he ruins in the process.

And he knows that I'm powerless to him. I've allowed myself to become sucked into his world more than I should have. He could have Rizzoli fire me. He knows where I live. He's Dean's father. Not to mention, he already threatened Cale.

I know he wouldn't kill me because then Dean wouldn't be as cooperate with his father. And Carlo still needs him.

"Go to hell," I tell him just before exiting. I race over to the entrance of my building, half expecting him or his driver to follow me, but they don't.

If he exposes me, I wouldn't have a way of denying his story. Not when I was the boy who was struck by lightning. Not with the lightning scar up my arm, just like the Fuse suit. Not without any solid alibis for my outings as Fuse.

With the public reception of Fuse the way it is thanks to the *Tribune*, it wouldn't be long before I'm arrested. My life, as I know it, would be over.

Chapter Thirteen

slam the door shut behind me after I enter the apartment.

"Your fucking father is spineless!" I bellow at Dean. He turns from his position on the couch with his eyebrows high and his eyes wide. His hand grips his lit-up phone.

"What's going on?" He stands and slips his phone in his pocket.

"He's so fucking paranoid that he's not even *listening*!"

"Listening's not really his strong suit."

I glare at him. "This isn't funny, Dean. He just told me that if I don't stop being Fuse, he'll kill Cale!" At this point, exposing me as Fuse is the least of my worries.

Dean raises his eyebrows again. "Wait, he just talked to you?"

"He was waiting on the street when I got home."

"And he said Cale was Fizz?"

"He made it pretty obvious that he knows."

"Oh."

"Dean, what if something else happens to Cale? I couldn't save him the first time, but I'm not going to let anything else happen to him. And did you see that there were *two* articles in the *Tribune* today that basically make me sound like a criminal? He's got the press completely wrapped around his finger, and I have no idea how I'm going to be able to get out of this without word getting out that I'm Fuse. I'll probably even get arrested. And what if something happens to Myra if I'm outed? She's going door to door in the most dangerous part of the city because she has no other option. All it'll take is one psycho to—"

"Okay, stop speculating. Things are different this time with Cale. We'll figure out a plan to make sure nothing happens to him. And the articles will blow over. They'll have someone else to write about tomorrow."

"Yeah, Myra. I can't let anything happen to her, either."

"Nothing's going to happen to her. She's tough. She can handle herself."

"What if she loses her job? Everything she's worked for will be gone because there are lies being spread about her."

"As long as she's doing her job, they have no reason to fire her. It's an elected position. She'd have to do something really bad to lose it. Besides, even if that *does* happen, she'll find something else."

"So conspiring with someone the paper deems a criminal like Fuse isn't bad enough to get her fired?" I shake my head. Everything seems to be hitting me at once. "Dean, I don't know what I'm going to do. He's untouchable. He's already gotten to Cale and is planning to do it again, he's defaming Myra, he's about to expose me, and he keeps pulling you closer. He's got a hook in everyone I care about. I'm really scared of what's going to happen."

Where will it end? If he kills Cale and outs me as Fuse, will Carlo stop there? Or will he continue on to my parents? Maybe even Alex and Wes for helping me? Since he needs Dean, Carlo might not be coming after me personally, but that doesn't mean he can't hurt the people around me to get me to back off as Fuse.

The more experienced I get as the man in black, the harder it is to remember the days when I didn't have to worry about all of this. Back before I was electrocuted. Back before I was in the snares of the Martelli crime family. Back before I lost some of the people closest to me.

Dean hugs me, and I wrap my arms around him and pull him closer.

"Ethan, I'm sorry," he says over my shoulder. "I'm sorry that this is happening to you. I'm sorry that you're scared. I'm sorry for whatever part I played in that. I'm done talking to my father. No more. I can see now that no good can come from it."

Well, that's a surprise. I pull away from him enough to look in his eyes. "What are you talking about?"

"I've been thinking since we talked yesterday. You're right. These favors he's having me do, the lunches, the phone calls, it's what he does to people he thinks are valuable but he can't quite trust yet. Newbies to his business. I've been down this road before. I know how it goes."

"What about having a relationship with your father?" I have to throw him a bone. Even though I hated how much time he's been spending with Carlo, it must've meant something for Dean. The fact that his father is poison has to sting, even a little bit.

"There wasn't ever a relationship there to begin with," he says. "Not really, anyway. Besides, you didn't like it and I should've respected that."

"Dean—"

His kiss silences me. It surprises me at first, but then I give in to it. Wrap my arms around him tighter. Other than the kiss last week, we haven't kissed or had any real physical contact since he told me he needed space. I have so many questions, but in the moment I ignore them all. Instead, I indulge in what I've wanted for months now and let him pull me to my room.

When we're close like this, Dean has a way of making me forget the world and all of my issues. All I can think of now is being with him, how much I care for him, how glad I am that he's here. That I'm not going through all of this alone. That even though I've lost a lot since I became Fuse, I found him along the way.

———

"WELL, THAT WAS a lot better than last time." We're lying against the headboard of my bed now, covered only by my comforter.

"You were more relaxed this time." Dean brings our interlocked hands up to his lips and kisses the back of mine. "You knew what you wanted."

My cheeks flush. "So what now?"

"What do you mean?"

"Where do we go from here?"

"With us or with everything else?"

I feel the heat in my face again. It's time to be honest. I hate being this vulnerable, but what we just did shows we've crossed that line from friends to more-than-friends. Again.

"Um…both, I guess," I say.

"All right. Let's start with us." Nothing like jumping right into the deep end.

"You told me that you weren't ready to be with me. What changed?"

He studies our interlocked hands and takes a deep breath. "I guess I've just been thinking about how even though I said I needed time…I don't know, you were still here. You were still looking out for me. You just wanted me in your life, and it didn't matter whether we were together or not." He laughs nervously. "Plus, you know, I'm on meds now."

I give him a goofy grin. "Aw, Dean!"

My heart is pounding in my chest from nerves and I try to play it off with humor. Still, what he said about meds—more importantly, the reason he's on them—needs to be discussed. Especially since that was the reason he put the brakes on us before.

"So we're uh, boyfriends now?" My face turns red and I look away.

He chuckles, just as red as I am. "If that's okay with you."

"Yeah. It's just a little weird."

"I know."

"So how are you with…what happened?"

He swallows hard. "That still bothers me. Especially because I don't know what happened before you got there. I've been dealing with it, though. I probably always will have to, but I can't let that dictate my life anymore. If I do, he still wins."

At a loss for words, I kiss his shoulder and let him talk.

"Besides, you've already waited this long. I can't imagine you'd stick around for much longer if I didn't give you something." He cracks a smile to lighten the mood.

"Dean, let's be serious here. I wasn't going anywhere. I told you so the other night."

"I know, but I just thought you'd find someone…"

I hook an eyebrow. "Now who's speculating?"

Worming out of my grasp, he pushes me flat on the bed and kisses me.

Dean's mine. It really feels like a weight has been lifted off of me now. Now I know I can trust him completely. He's not the type of person to use someone. If he's willing to be with me again, it means he's really on my side.

After a minute, I push at him and sit up. "Okay, we can do that in a bit," I say with my newly permanent smile. "Right now we need to talk about your father."

He sits up too and straightens out the covers. "Well, that's a mood killer."

"Tell me about it." I wonder if I could use Dean's renewed relationship with his father to get him to call off his threats. But Carlo would probably see right through that. Besides, I shouldn't use my relationship with Dean in that way.

"Well, the real problem with my father's paranoia is that he's afraid of Michael Bello. Or rather, the types of people he'll inspire to rise up against him. Whether it's Bello or someone else, my father's afraid of losing power."

"So what does that mean? Should we *actually* help Bello overthrow your father? If that happens, I don't think you'd be safe, being Carlo's son and all."

Dean shakes his head. "No, not that. We should be as hands-off as possible. If we could find Bello and convince my father to meet with him or one of the gang leaders he's been working through, then maybe they could come to some sort of truce."

"Those are some big ifs."

"Then maybe just establish boundaries or something. There needs to be some kind of resolution. These reactionary attacks out of fear or paranoia aren't getting anyone anywhere."

"Wouldn't any suggestion from you look like a direct response to his conversation with me? He knows we're together."

He smirks at me. "Yeah, we are kind of a package deal, aren't we?"

"Just a little."

He sighs. "Well…I'd have to spin it so it sounds like it'd be a benefit to him. Play up the depletion of resources and the risk of police involvement and all of that. Bello's been a part of the family operation since before I was born. He knows how to weaken my father's empire and he's doing it."

"Are you even in a position with Carlo to give a suggestion like that? Doesn't he make his own decisions?"

"He'd probably consult with Rizzo, but if I lead with reminding him of Rizzo's friendship with Bello, he may listen to just about anyone."

I narrow my eyes. "I don't know. Still seems like a stretch."

He shrugs. "Maybe I'll come up with something better." He notices my defeated mood. "What's the matter?"

"I'm just afraid that he's going to play along since he knows about us, and then use you as bait to get to me. Or worse, he might just—"

Dean shakes his head. "He wouldn't kill me."

"You said it yourself that he's dangerous. He had no issues with disowning you when you were younger."

"That was a long time ago. I think we've both grown past that."

This conversation is getting dangerously close to an argument, and I don't want to ruin the evening we've had so far. Luckily, I don't have to respond to him as my phone starts ringing on the bedside table.

"It's Wes," I tell Dean just before I answer. "Hello?"

"Mr. Pierce, hello. I hope I'm not calling too late."

I glance at the clock. Just after nine o'clock. "No, we were just, uh…hanging out." I watch as Dean pulls on his clothes and leaves the room. "What's up?"

"Dr. Fletcher and I have finally finished studying the sample you gave me from the Works."

"Oh yeah!" I'd almost forgotten about asking him to test the jar of chemicals. At this point, I already know what happened to Cale, but more information couldn't hurt. "What did you find?"

"Well, that's what I wanted to talk to you about," he says. "Dr. Fletcher and I have some concerns, and we'd like to discuss this in person."

Chapter Fourteen

Alex is quiet but has a disapproving look on her face as we wait for Wes to come down to the basement of the clinic. She hasn't said anything about our reason for meeting, but I can tell she has some opinions on it.

I sit quietly with my hands tucked under my legs. After what seems like a lifetime, Wes comes down the stairs.

"Sorry about the delay," he says. "My last patient had a lot of questions."

"It's okay," I tell him. "So…what did you find?"

He takes a seat at the computer chair and reviews the contents of a manila folder for a moment before starting.

"Well, thanks to my resources at OU, we found traces of sulfuric acid, hydrochloric acid, sodium hydroxide, lime, and silver nitrate in the sample. All of which line up with the chemicals found on Luca Martelli's body, according to the copy of the coroner's report you sent me."

"Interesting," I muse as my mind wanders. So Fizz spits the same chemicals found at the Works, further proving my assumptions that Cale is Fizz.

"Based off of what we found, as well as the recent murders at the hands of Fizz, I think it's safe to say he is quite dangerous," Wes continues. "Definitely someone who needs to be avoided."

"Or stopped," I add.

Alex narrows her eyes. "You're not thinking of hunting him down, are you?"

It's probably best not to tell her that I already know where he's staying. "Isn't it my job to protect the people of Olympia? If Fizz is killing people, I need to make him stop."

"Mr. Pierce, I really think you should reconsider," Wes says. "At the very least, reconsider going alone."

"I'll take Dean with me."

"The acid this Fizz creature produces would damage Mr. Martelli's skin just as much as it would yours," Wes says. I want to correct him that Dean's last name isn't technically Martelli anymore, but I let it go.

"I have to do something," I say.

"Ethan, why are you so adamant about looking into this Fizz creature?" Alex asks. "Aren't you more worried about the mob war?"

"I think they're connected."

They both look confused, so I elaborate.

"You know how my brother disappeared a few months ago? He was looking into the Works, trying to expose the massive cover-up, but the Martellis got to him first. They threw him in the vat…and he became Fizz."

Wes shakes his head. "Ethan, I think that's highly unlikely. What other evidence do you have that puts Cale at the Works that night?"

"I found a piece of his shirt where the chemical pool was," I start.

"And that proves it's Cale?" Alex asks skeptically.

"Well, I also found the room he's living in at the Works," I say. "It's filled with newspaper clippings about the Works, the Martellis, and Myra."

"Mr. Pierce, I don't think you should get your hopes up,"

Wes says. "Neither of those actually prove that this creature if your brother."

"Maybe not, but Fizz said he was thrown into the chemicals, and Carlo Martelli himself admitted to it."

Wes and Alex look at each other and then back to me.

"Wait a minute, you *talked* to them?" she asks. "What the hell were you thinking!"

"I was thinking that I found my brother after looking for him for *months*! I was thinking I could help him! I was thinking that I finally found one of the many people who were taken from me in the last six months! Don't I deserve that?"

They're both quiet after my outburst, so I continue in a softer tone.

"Look, I get that they're both dangerous. Believe me, I know Carlo is, but I think I can save Cale. There has to be something we can do to return him to the way he used to be. Right?"

Wes lets out a heavy sigh and tucks his hands in his pockets.

"Wes, tell me there's some way we can help my brother," I plead. "Isn't there a counter substance we can give him, or maybe some other form of treatment or something? He can't stay like this. Not because of Martelli."

"Mr. Pierce, there's nothing we can do to change his body back to the way it used to be," he starts.

I shake my head and get to my feet, looking away from them with my hands on my hips. This can't be. Cale deserves better than this. I can't leave him looking like he does now.

"Mutations are permanent," he continues. "Look at the way your own body changed when you were electrocuted. You'll never not be able to generate electricity. The same concept can be said for your brother's mutation. There's no going back to the men you used to be."

I turn and look at him, doing my best to keep the guilt from spilling out of my eyes. "Then how come I look the same as I did before I mutated and Cale looks like a freak?"

"I can't be certain, but based off of what you told me, his body was subjected to more severe extremes than yours was. Electricity and toxic chemicals are two very different entities, and your bodies reacted quite differently as well."

I'm at a loss for words, but luckily I don't have to come up with any, as my phone buzzes in my pocket. I answer it as an excuse not to have to say anymore on the subject of Cale.

"Hey, are you done at the clinic yet?" Dean asks.

"Just about, why?"

"Heard on the police scanner that there's a possible shooting at the Works," he says. "I think my father's keeping the promise he made you and he's going after Fizz—Cale, I mean. Sorry. Ethan, he's going to kill him."

I swallow the lump in my throat. That bastard can't even give me a full twenty-four hours before he moves in on my brother.

"Are you there?" he asks after a while.

"Yeah, I'm here. Can you come pick me up?"

"I'm already on my way down to my bike," he says. "See you in a bit."

I hang up and stare at my reflection in my blank phone screen.

"What's the matter?" Alex asks.

"Martelli's going after Cale," I say. "He told me that he'd kill him if I don't stop being Fuse."

"Why does he care about you being Fuse?" she asks.

"He thinks I'm working for Michael Bello. Dean's coming to pick me up."

"Mr. Pierce, I hope you'll be careful with Fizz," Wes says.

"Cale, you mean," I correct him.

"Right. Anyway, you may have mutated a bit from the lightning strike, but you're still human. If you want, I can stay in contact with you here in case anything goes wrong."

"No, that's okay. I don't want to get you guys involved any more than you already are." Besides, there's nothing they'd be able to do from the clinic if Carlo or one of his men get to Cale before I can save him. "Thanks for all your help."

Alex looks at me with sad eyes. "Ethan, are you okay?"

I shrug. "Not really, but I'll be fine."

She pulls me into a hug and mutters in my ear, "I know

this doesn't change things, but you're strong enough to handle something like this."

It doesn't feel like it. I'm doing my best to stay disconnected, to *not* think of Fizz as my brother. But despite my best efforts, that's all I can think of. And I know he's supposed to be the big brother, the one protecting me, but with all the power that I have, I can't help but feel like I've failed to protect him.

And now he's in danger. I have to save him.

———

GUNS FIRE AT us from two parked cars as Dean maneuvers the bike through an opening in the chain-link fence into the Works complex. He manages to get around the corner of one of the buildings and out of sight, stopping long enough for me to hop off, and then takes off back in the direction he came.

We've had our coms linked up since he picked me up at the clinic. We both know the plan. He's going to lead the lookouts away from the Works while I take care of the guys inside and get Cale to safety.

Smashing through one of the windows of the nearest building, I climb inside to get my bearings. As my eyes adjust to the darkness, the features of the room come into view. Looks like some sort of large storage room with long rows of empty shelves lined up. Running down the aisle, I find a door and step out into another cavernous warehouse.

This place is huge. Cale could be anywhere.

More gunshots fire, this time from the next room over. I hear Fizz's distinct roar and break out into a run toward the ruckus.

The next room is filled with conveyor belts and assembly line tables. On the other side of the room, my brother roars again and I creep through the defunct machinery to get closer to him.

Using the conveyor belts for cover, I listen as Cale and Martelli's men move throughout the room. I still haven't spotted my brother, which is good, but I know he's here.

"Get ready, boys," one of the men says from the other side of the machine I'm hiding behind. "This one's not going down easily."

A crash on the other side of the room draws our attention as my brother leaves through the door I just came through. Two men quickly follow him.

The remaining other two come around from behind the machine and seem just as surprised to see me as I am that they've suddenly spotted me.

We all jump into action quickly, both of them pointing their guns at me.

"Easy, Fuse," the one in a gray suit says.

I put up my hands in surrender, palms facing them.

"Nothing funny, got it?" the other one asks. He's in an all-black suit.

"Okay." Quickly, I shoot lightning out of my hands and hit them both squarely in the chest, sending them back onto the ground convulsing. Scooping up their guns, I throw them across the room and turn to follow where my brother and the two other men just went.

It's quiet in the next room, and I keep close to the wall since there's no other cover.

They have to be here somewhere. There are a couple doors they could've escaped through, one of them being the storage room I came from.

Moving along the wall, I begin to check each room until I hear gunshots from down below.

There must be a basement here, too.

I find the right door and jump down the steps to each landing until I've reached the bottom, the cement covered in a tar-like substance that sticks to my boots. It smells down here, too. And it's dark.

The flare from the gunshots comes into view a few feet away. I take a chance and send a streak of lightning in that direction. In the brief illumination, I see my brother's massive form hunched in the corner behind the stairs. The two men are facing the opposite direction, but quickly turn to face me after the lightning.

Chapter Fourteen

Sprinting out of the way, I narrowly miss more bullets as they bounce off the cement. It's still too dark in here to see them, so I wait for something to happen. My heart is pounding in my chest.

One of the men fires again, giving away their location, and I send another streak of lightning. But I miss my target and hit Fizz's arm instead.

He roars loudly, and one of the men screams next to me. A moment later, I hear heavy footsteps on the stairs and one of Martelli's men following. I chase up after them and send another streak of lightning at the remaining pursuer. He falls to the cement, shaking.

Fizz stares at me with fear in his eyes. It's just us now. Neither of us move as we take each other in from across the room.

I thought I'd be relieved when I spotted him, but instead I'm feeling nervous. Scared, almost. What if he hates me now because I zapped him? Does he realize it was an accident? What if he's mad at me for not saving him from becoming this monster? How am I going to tell him that I don't have a way to fix him?

I take a step forward, but a threatening growl escapes him and I stop in my tracks. His saggy eyes look at me terrified as he studies me. He turns to run, but I call out to him.

"Cale, wait!"

He stops, his back to me, but still doesn't say anything.

"I'm sorry for hitting you downstairs. I didn't mean to hurt you." I venture a step closer in the light and he looks over his shoulder to eye me suspiciously. "Are you…" I swallow the lump forming in my throat. "Are you Cale Pierce?"

His shoulders sag and he turns to face me again.

"You are, aren't you?" I press.

Slowly, he nods.

I step closer and pull off my mask. "Cale, it's me. Ethan."

He stares at me without a word, so I continue.

"I, uh, just found out for sure that this is—that you—that I confirmed what happened to you," I start. "I guess you got the short end of the stick when it comes to mutations."

He tilts his head to the side, confused.

I hold out my hand and let small streaks of lightning trickle between my fingers. He takes a step back and looks at me with wide, droopy eyes.

"It's okay." I cut the lightning. "I'm not going to hurt you. When I was electrocuted at Wyatt back in October, my body changed…kind of like yours did. You were right. I'm Fuse."

His saggy jowls sway when he opens his mouth. I flinch, but nothing comes out. No acid. No sound.

"You can't talk, can you?"

He shakes his head.

More sorrow fills me. Guilt, even. If I had known he was being attacked that night he became Fizz, would I have chosen to save him or would I still have gone after Dean? It's impossible to answer and impossible to change.

"You're probably wondering why I'm here. Why I tracked you down."

I look up at him, expecting some sort of reaction, but I don't get any. He just watches me, so I continue.

"I need your help. Carlo Martelli, the man who's responsible for what happened to you, is at war with Michael Bello. They're fighting for control of the city. Like it's theirs for the taking. You of all people know what it's like to feel powerless."

Cale bows his head and watches Martelli's fallen soldier.

"He knows who you are," I say. "He knows you didn't die like he intended. That's what these men tonight were here for. To kill you."

Another step closer.

"You need to find another place to stay. I don't know where, exactly, but I know it's not safe here. Not with Martelli still around. I think you can help me take him and Bello down."

He looks up at me.

"We need someone who will really scare them. Carlo's afraid of you, which is why he wants you dead."

He doesn't seem to have any sort of expression on his face, which isn't the best when he can't talk. But his reaction to this next part is crucial.

Taking a deep breath, I say, "I know you killed Luca Martelli and Leon Wallace. Probably because of the role they played in you becoming this…creature. But helping me could be your chance to make sure nobody else gets hurt by these men."

He turns away from me and looks toward the door. A refusal without words.

"Please, Cale. I need your help. Olympia is your home. These people take advantage of everyone. Look what they did to you… and Emma. You can still help."

He doesn't do anything for a long while, and I'm afraid he didn't hear me, but then he shakes his head no.

"No?" I ask. "Why not? Cale, this could be a big—"

The roar of Dean's motorcycle just outside stops me. Suddenly, his voice is in my ear.

"There's a couple of cops out front," he says. "Wrap it up and let's get out of here."

I look up to tell Cale to hide, but he's already gone.

Chapter Fifteen

My heart races as the city hall elevator climbs higher to Myra's office. I haven't been to see her in the daylight. Or even without a mask. Not in a while, anyway. I watch the digital display above the door and try to think of the best way to start the conversation. It's all I can do not to think about where Dean is right now.

With our other options depleted, we came up with a plan B for dealing with Martelli and Bello. It's risky and makes me very nervous because it endangers the people closest to me. Well, the ones I have left.

When the elevator lets me off on the right floor, I walk through the room full of cubicles to Myra's private office. I smile at the older woman sitting at a desk next to Myra's door as I approach.

"Excuse me," the woman says, "do you have an appointment with Miss Connors?" She tugs at the lapels of her white jacket and the gold necklaces over her black turtleneck shimmer in the light. This must be Myra's assistant. I've only ever talked to her on the phone. She's new. At least, new for Myra.

"Uh, no appointment. Myra's a friend of mine."

"Just a moment, please." The woman—Nancy, according to her nameplate—reaches for the phone and looks through the window into Myra's office. "There's a young man here to see you."

I see Myra's confused look until she spots me.

"Okay, I'll send him in," Nancy says just before hanging up. "Sorry about that. Can never be too careful with all these reporters lately," she tells me. "Go on in."

"No problem. Thanks," I say. When I step into Myra's office, I hook my thumb behind me and say, "She's quite the watchdog."

"Yeah." Myra bangs a stack of papers on her desk to straighten them and then slips the pile in a manila envelope. "She comes with the job. What's up?" She sets the folder in a basket marked "outgoing" on the corner of her desk.

I take a seat at the chair opposite her desk. "Well, I've been thinking about how you said you felt trapped in this office."

"Not trapped, just limited." She clicks around a bit on her computer. "And very busy."

"Either way, you're stuck, right?"

She narrows her eyes and glances over at me. "Yeah…"

"And then I thought about the way you exposed Lloyd's connection to Bello and the Martellis, which basically got you this job."

Turning her full attention to me, she asks, "What are you saying?"

"Outing Lloyd like that was a big move. Risky, sure, but it paid off. And I know there are no guarantees that risks will ever pay off—I mean, look at Cale—"

"Ethan," she interrupts. "What's your point?"

"I think you should continue following that trail."

"What trail?"

"The one that linked other people in this building to the Martellis. You found some questionable practices. People who had the same connections as Lloyd."

She rolls her eyes and turns away, but I press on.

"I'm willing to bet that's why they're so critical of you. They want to discredit you. It's the reason you're getting so much hate in the paper. They're afraid of you because you might actually call them out on their wrongdoings."

"Ethan…" She shakes her head but doesn't say anything more.

"No, listen. The only way they can fight back is to drag your name through the mud. And with the connections they have with Martelli, they can do it."

That came out a lot sooner than I expected. I thought I'd lean into the accusation a little more, especially now that my words just hang in the air without a response.

Finally, she collects some more papers and then looks straight at me. "I'm on city council now, Ethan. I'm busier than I was before. I have more important things to do than—"

"More important than making sure *everyone* in the city is as fairly represented as your district is now?" I cut in.

She drops her head, hit by my words.

"Be honest," I continue. "How many other councilmembers do you think have been to their districts to talk to their constituents about issues going on in the city? How many of them do you think actually care about the people they're supposed to be serving?"

"Some of them do," she mumbles.

"But not all of them. And I'm willing to bet that it goes beyond the council. Martelli probably has people in so many different departments, not only on city council, but in the justice system, law enforcement, everywhere. Myra, this is your chance to make a difference for the whole city. Not just Hopman."

She sighs and looks at me. "I don't know. I haven't had this position that long. Most people already don't like me because of the way I got here. Why would I want to stir the pot further?"

"Because it's the right thing to do. It's who you are. Myra, the people who are going to make the biggest fuss about this are probably the ones who are guilty."

"Yeah, maybe."

She seems guarded. Closed off. I'm afraid she's just telling me what I want to hear to get me to go away, but this is an important part of the plan. Simply getting rid of Carlo Martelli and

Chapter Fifteen

Michael Bello will not put a stop to their operations. We need to expose as many crooked people in this city as possible until the system is too weak to survive.

"What are you afraid of?" I ask. "Is it the *Tribune*? Let your actions tell the story."

"It's not the *Tribune*."

"Then what is it? Did you get yelled at here? What's going on? Why are you so reluctant to do this?"

"Because I don't want to end up like Cale!" She covers her mouth and looks down.

It hits me how pushy I was. I put myself in her shoes. She's a public figure. The stakes are higher for her and she's already under attack by the media.

After a minute, I say in a soft tone, "That's not going to happen, because we won't let them know it was you who put this all together."

"Who else would it be?" she asks in a whisper, meeting my eyes. "Everyone already knows I'm the one who found the dirt on Lloyd. Why wouldn't I be Suspect Number One if even more people at city hall got arrested for similar charges?"

"Because Michael Bello spilled his guts when he was arrested," I counter.

"Not if the *Tribune* or someone else finds out it was me." She reaches for her purse and digs through it until she snatches a photo and lays it on the desk for me to see. "This was taped to my door the other day."

It's a picture of a rotting black hand. Similar to the one Cale received in November just before he went missing. My mind races trying to figure out what they know about her. How they're going to get her. What I can do to protect her.

I should've had her move into Cale's old room so I could keep an eye on her. Should've paid closer attention to what she was saying in interviews, how the public was receiving her—most importantly, how Martelli was receiving her.

I should've been staking out her apartment, city hall, anywhere she spent time. I should've been more careful about what the Martellis were learning about her. I wonder how much they've studied her routines, if they've measured up the weak spots in her security.

I can't let anything happen to her too.

"What is it?" she asks, breaking into my thoughts. "Ethan, that look is scaring me. What is this? What do you know?"

I turn the picture over and read the back.

Do your job, sweetheart, and don't worry about the rest.

Short and sweet. Not a formally structured letter like the one Cale got. It doesn't matter. The message is the same.

"Cale got one just like this. Right before…"

She brings a hand to her mouth and leans back in her chair, the color drained from her face. She looks like she's about to cry. "I don't even know who left it. Are you sure this is legitimate? Should I go to the police? I thought it was just a mean joke. I didn't think…"

I shake my head and turn it facedown on the desk to hide the disfigured hand. "Don't freak out about this."

She leans forward and whisper-shouts. "How can I not freak out?"

"You'll be fine. They won't touch you. I'll make sure of it."

"How, Ethan? This is the mob. Look what happened the last time they targeted you. And—"

I stand and she gets up to hug me.

"Look, I know it's scary," I say over her shoulder. "*I'm* scared. But continuing your work on this case is the best path forward. I promise you that."

She pulls away. "I appreciate your faith in me, but I don't understand how you expect me to continue to do the very thing that would get me killed. Isn't that what this note is warning me about? I haven't even told the police about this. Short of them babysitting me everywhere I go, I don't know how else I can protect myself besides laying low. Do my job, just like the note says."

I clench my jaw, running out of ideas about how to convince her to do what I'm asking. What's right. As much as I hate to push her to do something she's not comfortable with, I know I have to.

"Myra, just trust me."

"Why are you so adamant about this? Ethan, I could *die*."

"You're not going to die."

"How can you be sure?"

"Just trust me."

"I'm going to need more than that if I'm going to risk my neck—literally. You're hiding something. Spill."

I run my hands through my hair and mutter, "I'm Fuse."

She sits back down in her chair and stares at me. Her brow is furrowed, and she seems to be trying to decide whether I'm telling the truth or not.

Meanwhile, I feel my face flush. I shove my sweaty hands in my pockets and wait for her response, completely exposed.

"Are you serious?"

I nod without meeting her eyes.

"Since your accident?"

"Yeah." My voice is small and my throat is dry. I lift my sleeve and show her the scar on my right arm.

She grabs my wrist and inspects it, then looks up at me. "Did Cale know?"

He does now. "No, he didn't know."

"How? I mean, you're not athletic or—" She looks away. "That came out wrong. What I meant is, you're not...you don't seem like the type of guy—is that why you started going to the gym?"

I smile nervously. "Yeah. Listen, I know you won't, but please don't tell anyone. Too many people already know. And after what they're saying about me—well, Fuse..." I shake my head. "I don't want to bring down your name any more than I already have."

She nods.

The clock shows 12:45. I'm going to be late getting back to work.

"I have to go," I announce as I step toward the door. "Just promise me you'll think about what I said."

She still looks shocked, but nods anyway. "I will, yeah."

Fuse: Oblivion

With another look in her direction, I head back downstairs, wondering if I just made one of the biggest mistakes of my life. Myra is about principles, and if she knows I'm Fuse and she believes I'm breaking the law in some way, she may have a moral obligation to tell the police what she knows.

But Myra's basically family. She wouldn't do anything that could hurt me anymore than I would try to hurt her. I just hope that's enough.

Chapter Sixteen

I greet Dean with a kiss when I walk in the apartment from work. "How'd it go with your father?"

He pulls me into a quick side hug as he stirs the pasta boiling on the stove. "Good. He liked the idea, actually."

"So is he going to set up a meeting?" My hand lingers on his back. Just because I can.

It's weird how quickly we've fallen into a relationship dynamic. What's weirder is how natural it feels. I suppose it's because we've been dancing around the elephant in the room for months, relying on each other's companionship without crossing the line into more-than-friends territory. We're way past that line now.

"Well, there's a catch. Since he thinks you're working for Bello, he wants me to persuade you to get Bello to the pump house at Terry Lake tomorrow at noon."

"Me? Tomorrow? That's so soon."

"Yeah," he continues. "It doesn't really leave us much time to prepare. I thought we'd have a night off to ourselves." He turns and kisses at my neck. I push him away with a laugh.

"Stop," I chuckle. "Let's focus. How are we going to get in touch with Bello? I'm not sure he's even in Olympia."

Dean nods. "I think he is. And he's using someone here to do his work for him. Haven't you found anything that indicates who his ringleader here is?"

"I mean, there were the men your father's crew was shooting at that night in Hopman. After we went to the morgue."

"Well, there's a reason my father was targeting them," he says. "Based off of previous experience, if my father has a hunch he's willing to act on, he's probably right."

"Okay, then I guess we're tracking them down tonight. But we also need to come up with a game plan for the meeting once we get in touch with Bello's people."

"You're right." Dean turns his attention to the sauce on the stove.

"Did your father seem surprised that you approached him about it?" I slide onto the barstool behind the counter.

"A little, but he didn't ask too many questions."

"What was your reasoning for bringing it up?"

"That the more power Bello gains, the greater chance everyone on my father's team has of going to prison because of what Bello told the police. If the mob war escalates, Bello could pull some strings remotely and set some of my father's men up to be arrested. Even me and you. All of us are at risk."

True. That's part of what's been stressing me out lately. I can't wait until this is all behind us. But then, with Dean's family being who they are, will it ever really be over?

"What did he say to that?" I ask.

He shrugs, his back turned to me. "Not much. Just that I had a point and it'd be better to take control and work out a resolution before it gets further out of hand."

"So he took the bait?"

"Yeah. Probably isn't surprised that I'd want to keep the peace."

"Yeah," I mumble.

My mind is turning. This plan is going so smoothly, other than the time it took to convince Myra. But I expected that.

Carlo jumping at the chance to talk to Bello? Seems too good to be true. Even if the catch is that I have to get in touch with Bello somehow. It's still fishy. But what other choice do we have but to move forward?

"What about Myra?" Dean asks, glancing at me over his shoulder. "Is she going to continue to look into people at city hall?"

I take a deep breath and let it out slowly. "I think so."

"That bad, huh?"

"Well, not exactly. Not really. I don't know."

"That's descriptive." He carries the pot of pasta over to the sink and pours out the steaming water.

"Someone sent her a Black Hand letter."

He turns and looks at me with wide eyes. "That's not good."

"No." I gather the newspapers and mail scattered across the counter and collect them in one pile. "And it's probably because he's mad at me. He went after Cale and now he's going after Myra. She's freaked out. I'm freaked out too."

"So what did you say to calm her down?"

"I told her she had nothing to worry about."

"And that worked?"

"No." I play with the corner of one of the newspapers. "I had to tell her I'm Fuse."

"What?" The pot cover falls to the counter with a clatter. "Why? How did that even come up?" He leans against the island to face me.

I shrug. "I don't know. I was trying to convince her to keep digging but she wasn't really listening and had a bunch of perfectly valid excuses for why she should stop. She wasn't convinced she'd be protected. Not after Cale. So I told her I'd protect her as Fuse. I can trust Myra."

Dean pulls two bowls from the cupboard and begins filling them. "Isn't that also putting her in a tight spot if she's ever questioned about her relationship with Fuse?" he asks. "Before, she could honestly say she didn't know who he was. Now, someone might pick up on the fact that she's lying. With the way things are, they'd eat her alive."

He sets a bowl in front of me and comes around to the barstool beside me to dig in to his.

"I never thought of that," I admit.

I pull the bowl toward me as I replay the conversation from my lunch hour in my head. It happened so quickly. I didn't have time to consider all the variables. I should have. We're already messing up the very delicate plan.

"She might refuse to tell me things going on with the city because she knows who I am. She did that with Cale."

"That was different. A reporter has to cite his sources. Fuse doesn't." Dean points to my bowl. "Eat your food before it gets cold." When I pick up my fork, he continues, "Without anyone else knowing you're Fuse, the fact that she's providing you with information won't be an issue. Especially if she believes it'll be put to good use."

"Yeah, maybe. But your father knows I'm Fuse. And if he's already targeting Myra—"

"My father hasn't told anyone in his camp that you're Fuse."

"How do you know?"

"Because he told me."

"And we can take his word for it?"

"He agreed to meet with Bello at my suggestion, didn't he?"

"Okay, but what if Myra isn't convinced?" I ask. "I didn't get a chance to talk to her about my confession before I left. What if she's having second thoughts about pursuing the case?"

"If you want, I could help her point out certain people I know who have been in contact with my father. I mean, it's been awhile since I've really been involved with my father's operations, but loyalty is kind of a big deal with him. Unless one of them crossed him, he'll still be in touch with them. And some of these positions with the city have been years in the making."

I consider that. It's not a bad idea to have Dean help Myra. It would definitely save her time looking for the right people to dig into. Dean might even be able to offer her some sort of clue as to what their ultimate motive is.

"Maybe that'll work," I tell him. "Except, then she'll know

you're Martelli's son. I'm not sure how she'd take that. She's only met you a few times."

He offers a smile. "I'll just have to win her over, then."

———

THE ATMOSPHERE OF Myra's office is quite different from when I visited it at lunch earlier today. Almost everyone is gone—including Nancy—and most of the lights are off except the one in Myra's office. Actually, this is the way I'm used to seeing it since I've been here so often as Fuse.

When Dean and I step through her door, I spot a sub wrapper spread out in the corner of her desk. Dinner, apparently. She's focused on her computer screen at the other end of her desk. Her eyes flicker up to us.

"Give me just…one…second…" Her hands hover over the keyboard as she finishes typing. When she's done, she clicks on a few things before turning to us, her eyes lingering on her screen for a moment before looking at me with a smile. "Back again?"

I grin. "You're just so irresistible, Myra."

She rolls her eyes, still smiling.

"You remember Dean, right?"

"Sure, yeah." She stands and shakes his hand before we each sit down.

"Working late?" I ask.

"Yeah. The routine stuff usually takes the majority of my day. After hours is about the only time I'm able to get ahead of the game and work on kick-starting activity in my district."

"Any luck?"

She shrugs. "Same old, same old. Tonight I've been emailing the few business owners and church leaders to try to get some sort of community event planned. Money is the issue, though."

I nod. "Mm-hmm."

"What about you?" she asks. "What brings you back down here?"

"Well, I thought Dean would be able to help you with what we talked about earlier," I say. "The, uh, case against some of your coworkers."

She sucks on her bottom lip and nods once.

"I'm sure you know of my father," Dean adds. "Carlo Martelli."

Her eyes grow wide and she looks between the two of us, still without a word. Internally, I cringe. That was not the way I intended to deliver that piece of information. I'm glad we shut the door behind us.

"They're not—Dean's not working with him," I add quickly. "He hasn't really talked with his family since he was a teenager."

"Mmm." Myra balls up her sub wrapper and tosses it in the trash, avoiding eye contact.

"Ethan told me how you were considering digging deeper into my father's connections with elected officials, and I just thought I could help," Dean says. "It's been awhile, but I should be able to pick out names."

She continues to fuss with tidying up her desk, gathering papers, straightening pens, even refilling the stapler. A conscious effort not to make eye contact.

I watch her for a minute before asking, "So…what do you think? I found some of Cale's notes he took on the Works. What he was going to use for his story. I don't know if there are any leads in there, but it might be a place to start."

Banging another stack of papers on her desk to straighten them, she lays them flat and says, "Ethan, can I have a word with you outside for a minute? It'll just be a second."

"Uh…sure, yeah. No problem." I shoot Dean a look before following her out the door.

She keeps her hand on the doorknob and leans in close to me to whisper. I can tell she's not very happy.

"Are you *kidding* me?" she whispers furiously. "You had a member of the Martelli family *living* with you for *months* and you haven't gone to the police yet?"

"Myra, he's not—"

She rolls her eyes. "Yeah, yeah, he's not working for them

anymore. Doesn't mean he's not still dangerous. *If* what he says is true."

"He is—"

She shakes her head. "I don't buy it. And if you think *I'm* going to start working with him, then you've lost your damn mind."

"He's not like his father. We can trust him. I *know* we can."

"And why's that? How do you know he's not like his father? Does he know your secret? Are you sure he's not running along and reporting everything he learns about you to Daddy Dearest? Ethan, I have a lot on my plate right now and I'd appreciate you not adding any more to—"

"Dean and I are dating." It comes out louder than I expect, and my jaw clenches as I hear my words echo throughout the open office. There are still a few people here, and I know they've heard. We probably already had their attention from our whispered argument.

"Oh." The confession seems to disarm her, and she lets out a deep breath of air. "Lots of confessions today…"

"Yeah. It's still pretty new—really new—but I believe him when he says he's not working with his father. I brought him here so he could help. This could be potentially dangerous for him too."

She presses her palms to her forehead. "Wait a minute, back up. When did this happen? Is that why he moved in? Did Cale know? When did you—how did you—spill."

I smile nervously. "It's only been *official* since yesterday."

She rolls her eyes and crosses her arms, waiting for further explanation from me.

"But," I add quickly, "we were sort of…together before that. Not long. After Emma. I wasn't cheating on her. It's just—I don't know. Dean is different. Important. To me, at least. I need you to give him a chance. He's only trying to help."

Casting a glance through the window into her office, she says, "Okay. Fine. I'll see what he has to say. But I'm still not comfortable with this, Ethan. Not after everything that's been said about me lately. Your relationship status doesn't change anything."

I nod. "I know. Hopefully this will all be resolved soon."

It has to be.

Fuse: Oblivion

———

MYRA WASN'T HAPPY about me leaving her alone with Dean. I tried my best to assure her that she had nothing to worry about, but she still wasn't convinced. I feel bad, but I don't really have time to worry about it. I have other things to do if we're going to keep this plan in motion and get Bello to the meeting place tomorrow.

After leaving city hall, I went to the clinic to search for anything on the gang Martelli was targeting in Hopman. Out of the surviving gang members, Kendrick Jackson, appears to be the one who took charge after former gang leader Miguel Wilson was killed in the shootout.

Since then, not only has Jackson tried to kill my brother, but he's also been suspected of breaking into Joe Gotti's casino before the raid while still keeping up with his drug rings in Hopman, according to the police file on him. The OPD hasn't moved in on him yet because they believe he's in contact with Michael Bello and want to see if Bello will show up in Olympia.

Obviously, he's the one I'm tracking down now.

Jackson's legal address is at 153 Adams Street, but the place is empty when I get there. There are minimal signs that it's been lived in: a mattress in each bedroom upstairs, beer bottles lined up on the kitchen counter, working electricity. The question is, Where is he now?

I consider waiting for him. It's almost midnight, and these are probably his busiest hours. He's sure to turn up by daylight. But by then it'll be too late for him to get in touch with Bello to get him to Terry Lake in time for the meeting.

Hitting the com in my ear, I call over to Dean at city hall.

"Hey, see if you can pull up the address for Miguel Wilson from the Grid," I say. "Myra should be able to access it."

"Uh…just a sec," he says just before relaying the message to Myra. "No luck so far?"

"No, but I've only been to one guy's house. What about you guys?"

"Making a lot of progress, actually."

"Well, that's good to hear."

"Yeah. Okay, Miguel Wilson's address is 34 Canal Street. Is that close to you?"

"Yeah, it's not far," I say. "Thanks. I'll be in touch if I need anything else."

"Be careful."

Back out on the street, I run through the shadows toward Canal. Somewhere, Jackson is running his operations. If it's not his house, then it must be Wilson's house, who he took over for. Trouble is, he's not likely to be the only one there.

It's not hard to spot which house it is, because it's the only one with a light on behind the curtained windows at this hour. I crouch on the side of the rotting porch in the shadows and try to come up with a plan. I have to assume that he and anyone with him are armed, which means I need to draw the others out before I go in.

I could fire a bolt of lightning inside the window, possibly setting the house on fire, but that seems like it would cause more problems for bystanders than it would help me. Instead, I eye up the sleek sports car parked on the street. It's far enough away from any buildings that it wouldn't cause further damage.

Peeking around the porch, I zap the grill of the car. It only takes a quick jolt before flames erupt from beneath the hood.

A few minutes later, several men run out from inside, one of them shouting, "My car! What the fuck happened to my car?"

Crouching low below the windows, I sneak around to the back door. There's a man out there smoking, facing inside the house to question the commotion out front.

Quickly, I punch him in the gut and flip him over the fence into the long-dead flower garden beside the back.

I step into the kitchen, which is empty. Most of the guys are out front, but I still don't see Kendrick Jackson among them. Finding the stairs, I slip up them and come face to face with another one of Jackson's friends. He grasps for the gun in his pocket, but I punch him before he has a chance and then push him down the stairs.

I navigate through the narrow hallway, searching the nearly

empty bedrooms until I come to the larger one at the end of the hall.

Jackson's there with another guy. The front window is open, but they're facing my way when I step through.

The other guy fires and I tuck back into the hallway just in time.

"I need to talk to Kendrick Jackson!" I shout.

"Fuck off, Fuse!"

"You're in touch with Michael Bello, aren't you? I need you to give him a message!"

"Who says I know anything about Bello?"

"You're working for him, aren't you?" I try to peek around the corner again, but his friend fires another shot. I hear the guys who went out to look at the burning car start to come back inside. I can't waste any more time.

Jackson's silence is enough of a confirmation for me. Throwing my hand back into the room, I send a streak of lightning in their direction. Just enough to distract them so I can get inside without getting my head blown off.

"Yo, KJ! We gotta get going! The suits are comin'!" one of the guys calls up the stairs. I hear the sound of fire trucks in the distance.

Kendrick and his buddy are both crouched on the ground. Before Jackson's friend can raise his gun, I strike him with my lightning again and leave him shaking on the floor. Meanwhile, I can feel myself start to weaken. Too much energy used so far tonight.

"What the fuck, man?" Jackson asks. He has a red bandana tied around his head and wears an oversized gray hoodie.

"He's up here! It's that Fuse guy!" someone calls from down the hall.

I shut the door, grab Jackson by the front of his hoodie, and slam him against the back of the door.

"Don't shoot!" he shouts. "Don't fucking shoot!"

I pound my fist into his chest, sending a trickle of electricity with it. "Tell your friend Michael Bello to be at the pump house in Terry Lake tomorrow at noon. He's going to come to a truce with Carlo Martelli."

"Like hell he is!"

I punch his chest again, releasing more electricity. "If he doesn't show, I'm coming for you."

Releasing him, I slip out the open window onto the mossy roof. Hopping down onto the grass, I note that most of the other men have gone back inside or fled from fear of the sirens. I take advantage of the moment and run into the night.

Chapter Seventeen

W e probably should get ready," Dean tells me the next morning.

"Yeah, I suppose so."

We've already been to the gym, and I've been stalling, opting to lay on the couch and play on my phone instead of going over our plan.

Dean and I both called off of work today. I've never done that for Fuse-related stuff, but I just couldn't pass up this opportunity to get both Martelli and Bello in the same room.

"Come here and take a look at this map real quick." He's got the satellite view of Google Maps pulled up over the park around Terry Lake, the namesake for Olympia's most-populated suburb.

When I come up behind him, he points to the screen. "This is where the meeting's taking place."

It's an old pump house that was built in the early 1900s. Kind of surprising that the building hasn't been remodeled into something different since Terry Lake is a wealthy community, but at the moment it's sitting empty. Well, until Martelli and Bello get there.

Now's our chance to get Bello back into police custody and finally get Martelli arrested. Hopefully it'll give us—and this city—some reprieve from the venom they've spread throughout Olympia. If we mess this up…well, hopefully we won't.

"They're not going to be alone," he continues.

"They're not? How do they have a civilized conversation with weapons raised?"

"Well, they'll be alone *inside*, but the outside will be guarded," he explains. "Not too heavily, to avoid suspicion, but we won't exactly be able to walk through the front door."

I have my doubts that Martelli and Bello will even come to a truce. The war didn't last that long, and both of them want the same thing: control over Olympia. The fact that they're former allies just adds fuel to the fire. That's if Kendrick Jackson actually got the information to his boss in time and if Bello even agreed to come.

"Okay, so we just need to get inside undetected. How sure are you that there won't be any guards inside?"

"I'm positive. It'll just be my father and Bello. They *may* each have one associate with them, just as a witness to their agreement, but they're not there to protect them in case of an attack. It's really just a matter of making sure there's not a he-said-she-said fight later, you know?"

I nod. "How many times has a meeting like this happened?"

Dean rocks his head back and forth while he thinks. "It's not too common, but it has happened. The last one was back when my father first became boss. Back when my family wasn't the only crime family in Olympia."

"Your father wiped them out?"

"Yeah. Or took over their operations."

"So why would anyone agree to meet with him if he basically took over the whole city?"

"Well, these meetings are different. It's at a neutral location—which is why it's at Terry Lake—and only the two men negotiating and their witnesses are allowed in the room and they don't come out until they agree on a deal. After that, the war is over."

"So it's just that easy?"

"I mean, these debates can last a long time, but that's the code."

"Still seems too good to be true."

"No, what seems too good to be true is the second part of our plan."

"You mean the part with Myra?" I ask.

"Yeah."

"You don't think she'll pull through?"

Dean says they accomplished a lot last night. I feel pretty good about it. He was home before me and said they dug through files, pulled up accounts and documents that looked suspicious, and added it all to the case.

"I know she will," he says. "I gave her a lot of dirt on my father's men. I just hope that he doesn't sweet-talk his way out of it. Then it would come back to bite us in the ass. This is pure violation of omertà."

"Yeah, I thought of that. But we just have to hope that Myra will pull through for us."

"Well, I pointed out a lot of names on the city's payroll that were acquaintances, or good friends, with my father, and that's the list we used to springboard the investigation," Dean says. "Some of the names didn't have anything questionable in their records, but that could just mean they've covered their tracks well. Myra still thinks we found enough to develop solid cases against fourteen people.

"In any case, we should probably get going. Meeting starts in an hour, and I want to get in position as soon as possible."

After I've pulled on my Fuse suit and Dean's loaded up with weapons, we head down to the parking garage and take off out of the city.

As we ride, I think of everything that was thrown at Myra yesterday. There's still a lot of work to be done before the case is presented to the police, but she seemed confident she could do it. She even told Dean that he saved her a lot of time. I guess knowing where to look was half the battle.

We park Dean's bike a couple blocks away from the park,

take a position behind the Terry Lake Clubhouse, and look down at the ornate pump house on the lake. Seated at the top of the hill overlooking the park, the clubhouse provides the best view. It also helps that it's still closed for the winter season.

Down at the pump house, several guards from both Martelli's and Bello's crews are standing outside the door. The difference between the two is obvious: Martelli's men are all well-dressed white men in suits and ties, while Bello's men are all different ethnicities and wear hoodies, jeans, and jackets. Clearly, Bello pulled these guys from his gangs in Hopman. I don't see Kendrick Jackson, so he must be inside with Bello.

"What do you say?" I mutter to Dean. Even though it's gloomy, it's still daytime, which I hate. My suit is designed to hide me in darkness. I'll have no cover here.

He points down to the crowd. "The windows are all barred, so we can't get in through there. And unless we want to jump in the water and crawl up through the machinery—which they might turn on if they hear us coming—we have to go through the front entrance."

"Great. Do you think we can take them?"

He nods and double-checks his ammunition for the third time. "You ready for this?"

"As ready as I'm going to be. Are you?"

"Same as you."

"You sure?" I ask. "If this doesn't go our way, you're as good as dead for violating omertà. We both are."

"I know. But we'll be fine."

It's a long shot, but the plan is to get inside and get Martelli, Bello, and their men tied up and ready for the police to come in and arrest them. Hopefully Myra finishes her cases in time for the police to charge them with something before they're forced to let them go.

I look down the hill again. "Looks like there are about ten men guarding the door. Our approach is critical to not getting killed. I'll zap something on the far side to distract them. When they go to check it out, we'll come in from this side. I'll cover you while you unlock the door."

He shakes his head. "Not all the guys are going to fall for that. We'll have to fight some off."

"I know, but we'll just have to do the best we can. You ready?"

He nods.

Stretching my arm out, I let electricity erupt from my open palm to a tree on the other side of the pump house. Four men, two from each side, run toward the tree to check it out. Meanwhile, Dean and I sprint down the hill to our target, trying to stay hidden among the trees as best we can.

One of Bello's men, who I recognize from the Wilson house last night, sees us and struggles to pull his gun from the pocket of his oversized black hoodie. I reach him before he gets it free, popping him right in the face with my fist and knocking him out.

Before I have a chance to catch my breath, I feel hands grab my arms and pull me off my feet, lifting me in the air, my back pressed against my attacker's chest. I struggle, kicking my feet out until they make contact with someone's face. What I presume to be a nose crunches under my boot.

A few gunshots fire around me. I ignore them, too focused on getting myself free. My attacker sets me back down on my feet after I get too heavy for him to hold, but keeps his arms locked around me. I drop my hand to whatever part of him I can reach and zap him with enough electricity to leave him convulsing on the ground.

Too much energy. I need to save my strength for when I'm inside. It doesn't help that I didn't get a full night's sleep last night.

The four men who chased after my distraction are back. They join the group of several men punching and kicking at Dean. One of them pulls a gun out, but I zap him before he has a chance to fire it.

My body weakens a little more, but it's worth it. I dive into the throng, punching at anyone still taking cheap shots at Dean. He's curled on the ground protecting himself, but once I pull some of the men off of him, he springs to his feet. His mouth is a little bloody and he has several bruises forming, but he wipes away the blood.

"You good?" I ask him.

"Yeah. So much for our plan, though."

"Pretty stupid coming here," one of the guards says. He's well-dressed. One of Martelli's men.

"Let us in, Donny," Dean demands.

Several of the men behind him chuckle. Now that many of them are hurt, the fighting has stopped for a moment.

"Easy, Dino. No need to be alarmed." Donny raises his hands in mock defense. "It's just a civil discussion between two very powerful men."

"And one of them is my father," Dean says.

"Is he? Last I knew you were no longer a part of this family. You can thank your boyfriend Fuse for that."

Dean raises his fist, and before I have a chance to stop him, several of the men grab me from behind and restrain my hands behind my back with zip ties so tight I feel them cut into my skin. I have flashbacks to when I was in a similar situation several months ago—at the hands of Bello. Back then, Dean came just in time to free me. But now I see he's being tied up by Donny the same way I am. No one to save us now.

A big guy in a torn suit grabs my arm and leads me inside. Luckily, Dean's right by my side being pushed by Donny. Better for us to be together than apart now that our plan has unraveled. It wasn't well-executed. It was rushed. We weren't prepared and we were sloppy. Not to mention outnumbered. Hopefully we can still get out of here. We've been in worse situations before.

Once we get past the doors and into the pump house, I see Martelli and Bello waiting for us. Bello looks quite different. His hair is long and curly, and he seems to have lost a lot of weight. His sunken face is hidden behind an unruly beard. Probably his disguise after escaping custody.

Martelli and Bello are seated at a large table in the middle of the room. Several smaller tables are pushed against the walls along with some chairs and wooden barrels. Some cardboard boxes are stacked against the ancient machinery. This place clearly hasn't been used in a long time.

What's most striking, though, is that Martelli and Bello are sitting next to each other behind the table, both sneering at us as we walk in. Rizzoli and Jackson are standing off to the side, their hands behind their backs.

Something isn't right. They don't appear to be in the middle of a discussion. They look like they're waiting for us.

Fear strikes through me that maybe all of this was a ruse to get to us. Maybe it was just one big trap that we were drawn into like moths to a flame. And it worked. Just like they wanted it to. I feel so stupid.

Maybe there wasn't even a rivalry to begin with.

Chapter Eighteen

W elcome, boys," Carlo Martelli says with a smile. He gets up and comes around the table. "We were wondering how long you'd last against our guards."

My heart pounds in my chest and I struggle against the guard's grip, but he's bigger than me. I don't want to take my eyes off of Martelli and Bello, so I can only imagine the look on Dean's face. Even if he's hiding it, he's probably feeling a mixture of panic, betrayal, and overall disappointment.

"Your boy looks a little roughed up." Bello stands and comes to the side of the table, keeping some space between them.

Martelli shrugs. "I guess he just doesn't have it in him. What can you do?"

"We could have a little fun with them. Make them scream a little." Bello looks right at me, and I can tell he's thinking about what happened to Emma.

By the look on Martelli's face, it's clear he doesn't like Bello's suggestion.

"No, we're not torturing my boy. No matter how much of a traitor he is." Martelli glares at Dean. "Even after I accepted him

159

back into my empire."

In my mind, I can almost hear the seconds ticking away until we're dead. I have to do something. Anything.

"Why are you doing this?" I ask Martelli. "He's your son. You've been protecting him. You even shot one of your own for him. Why would you turn on him?"

"What other choice do I have? He turned on me." His glance shifts over to Dean. "How is Ms. Connors doing, boy? You had an awfully long chat with her last night, didn't you? Spilled some secrets, perhaps? The same ones that put me in hot water for Frank Lloyd?"

I glare at him as he sneers at his son.

"And you," he says, turning to me. "We've already discussed your betrayal, but let's remind the room how you helped the police arrest Joe Gotti."

"That's me, not Dean," I say. "You don't know what he discussed with Myra!"

He nods. "True, but I think I can connect the dots just fine. Is that what I get for giving him a second chance? He knew what the risks were."

"You're disgusting," I say. "There shouldn't be any strings attached with family."

Carlo laughs. "That's just it! No family member of mine would break omertà."

"Go to hell," I tell him.

Martelli's face drops. "That's a shame. Not too long ago I thought that you could be very useful to me. Especially with your relationship with my son."

Bello looks between Martelli and me and Dean. "Relationship? Are you—" He breaks out in a fit of laughter. "Are you—" More laughs. "Are you two...*together*?" He's doubled over now, holding the table for support.

I scowl at him, even though he can't see it through my mask. I'm sure Dean's doing the same. At least, I hope he is.

"That's enough," Martelli declares, no hint of a smile on his face.

Bello wipes at his eyes, his shoulders still shaking. He points between the two of us. "Okay, but I have to know. Which one of you is, you know, the *boy* and which one's the *girl*?"

I take a step forward, but the guard yanks me back, the ties digging deeper into my wrists.

"How did you even know we were coming?" Dean asks.

Martelli steps slowly toward him and puts a hand on his shoulder. "My boy, you've never come to me to talk business before. When you suggested I make peace with Mikey, that's when I knew something was off. You wouldn't voluntarily talk business if you didn't have something planned. And do you think I wouldn't have assumed that you'd plan something Mr. Pierce here? I was counting on it. Why do you think I had him get in touch with Bello? I could've figured out a way to contact him myself."

Bello chuckles beside Rizzoli. "I still can't get over it. I mean, I guess I should've known. Dino has always been a little—"

"Since when are you two friends?" I ask Martelli to shut Bello up. I can't stand to listen to him anymore. "You just spent the last few weeks fighting him. Now that you have a common enemy you're friends?"

"Oh, make no mistake, Mr. Pierce. We're not friends." Martelli pulls a gun from inside his breast pocket, turns around and shoots.

But it's not Bello who cries out and tips over one of the tables as he falls clutching his injury.

It's Frank Rizzoli.

The echo of the gunshot rings in my ears so that I can barely hear Bello shout, "What the fuck?" as he points his own gun at Martelli. He takes a careful step closer to Jackson.

The guard holding me loosens his grip to reach for his weapon.

Martelli lifts his gun toward Bello.

"Why'd you shoot me?" Rizzoli grunts, still cringing with pain.

Martelli steps around the large table closer to him, keeping his gun pointed at Bello. "You think I'm stupid, don't you? That I'm getting up in age and losing my touch? My boy isn't the only one who has betrayed me, Frankie. I know *you've* been aiding my opponent for some time now. And don't think I don't know about your deal with the cops!"

The cops?

Martelli shoots a deadly look in Bello's direction. "You're both traitors." He turns back to Rizzoli. "You've been acting differently the last few months. More careful, less willing to act. Just as long as you don't get your hands dirty to avoid jail time, huh?"

My heart pounds in my chest. So Rizzoli also made a deal with the police? Is it the same deal Bello got? Why wasn't Rizzoli put in protective custody?

"You're working whatever angle you can to get the best deal for yourself," Martelli continues. "You thought I was blind to it all. But there's a reason I'm in this position. I notice things. I *remember* things. You and Mikey here were always a lot alike. And now it makes sense. Omertà means nothing to either one of you."

"You fucker." Bello shifts his aim and shoots at Dean.

"No!" I shout out, struggling against Martelli's guard as I try to step toward Dean.

His guard loosens his grip as Dean slinks to the ground, blood beginning to stain his pant leg. With his hands tied behind his back, all he can do is wince and roll to his side.

There's no way he's going to be able to walk by himself, let alone run. How are we going to get out of here now?

"Dean, are you okay?" I ask.

The guard holding me yanks me back as another gunshot fires. Soon the whole room erupts in them and the guard's hold on me weakens. Men from both sides are flipping over tables for coverage. The doors fling open as the rest of the guards from outside rush in, taking cover with their allies.

My captor tries to pull me toward Bello's side, away from Dean, but I squirm out of his grasp. Dropping to the floor, I kick out his feet and he falls. Turning so my back is to him, I shoot lighting out of my bound hands until I see his legs tremble from the corner of my eye.

Slinking to the ground again, I assess what's going on with

everyone else. The shots firing across the room tells me that they're all too preoccupied with each other to notice that I've overpowered the guard. So much for calling a truce.

I scurry over to Dean, who's still on his side, blood soaking his pant leg. He's half hidden behind a fallen stack of chairs, but it's not good enough cover.

"You okay?" I ask again.

He grits his teeth. "Hurts like a bitch. But yeah, I'll live."

"Hold on." I return to the guard I shocked and awkwardly try to search him for a knife or anything sharp to untie us.

Nothing.

I narrowly dodge a bullet as I return to Dean's side.

"Can you move at all?" I ask him.

He tries pushing at the floor with his good leg but doesn't get very far before he groans and slips back down. "Fuck!"

I look out the open door and see several men shooting from their positions out there. Not all of them rushed in, apparently. Bad men inside, bad men outside. We're stuck in here because Dean can't—

A bullet lodges itself in the wall behind us. We're too exposed where we are. Even if I just get him against the wall, that'll shield us a little better.

Looking around for anything that could help free us, I see a knife slide across the floor. I follow its path and my eyes meet Rizzoli's. He gives me a nod.

I'm stunned for a second but don't waste any more time as I snatch the knife up to free Dean. It takes awhile, given the angle—much longer than I want it to with the bullets flying through the air—but I get it.

Once free, Dean backs into the corner using both hands and his good leg, wincing and clenching his teeth the whole time.

"Let me see." He waves his fingers toward the knife.

I turn and let him cut me free, hoping nobody takes advantage of my moment of weakness.

Rizzoli sits back at the far wall near the ancient water pump and the stack of boxes that now have several bullet holes in them. His trail of blood indicates the path from where he was shot.

Martelli ducks for cover behind the old wooden table to the side. It also has several bullet holes in it. Two guards continue to shoot across the room beside him.

Bello is on the opposite side of the room using old wooden barrels for protection. I notice Jackson's limp body bleeding out onto the concrete floor next to the overturned table. There's only one other companion with Bello shooting at the opposite side.

Several other men lie dead in the center of the room—both the thugs and Martelli's made men. I see Donny among the fallen. Blood is splattered everywhere, and a muffled ringing sound fills my ears in place of the relentless gunshots.

My hands feel relief and Dean mutters, "There!"

There are likely bruises—if not cuts—along my wrists under my sleeves, but I ignore them. At least I can move again. Turning back to Dean, I ask, "Are you going to be okay here for now?"

He nods, and I turn to try to spot a free gun lying among the bodies for Dean to use. Nothing, so I decide to keep my position. Grabbing one of the bullet-ridden barrels still stacked against the wall, I position it in front of Dean and duck behind it for my own cover.

I zap the men shooting from outside first. They have the easiest getaway. Quick bursts of lightning, one after the other. They all drop, none of them dead, just exhausted. I'm sure the police are on their way now anyway, with what this meeting turned out.

Turning my attention to Bello's side of the shootout, I stand and raise my hand to zap his guard but feel a bullet graze my forearm, drawing blood. Immediately I drop back behind the barrel and assess my wound. Nothing too bad, but I'll probably need stitches.

Just as I summon the courage to try attacking again, the sudden silence makes me stop. Everyone's eyes are turned toward the entrance as Fizz shuffles through the door, droopy face, saggy skin, and all.

Quiet anticipation fills the room as everyone awaits his next move.

Suddenly, a gun fires from my left and I dive backward to cover Dean as best I can.

Chapter Eighteen

My brother roars and sprays deadly acid all over Martelli's men, who try to cover him. The holey table doesn't do much to protect them from the acid. One of the guards receives the full extent of the spray right in his face, while the one who dove on Martelli gets hit all over his back. It doesn't take long before both men's clothes disintegrate and their skin begins to melt off their bodies.

Dean pushes at me to try to get me off of him, but I hold my place. I don't know if Martelli is hurt, but right now there's nothing we can do for him. Especially Dean.

More gunshots fire, but they have no effect on Cale. Bello and his last remaining bodyguard use the moment of chaos to flee. They make it to the door before his companion is struck with Fizz's acid. Bello manages to slip by without even slowing for his lost guard.

"Go!" Dean tells me with a push.

I hesitate.

"I'll be fine! Don't let him get away!"

With Fizz now facing Martelli, I book it out of the pump house in pursuit of Bello. He's fast, but I don't need speed.

Raising my hand, I feel a numbness in the tips of my fingers from the loss of blood. But that doesn't stop me from shooting a streak of lightning toward Bello, feeling it drain from my body as it makes contact with him. He stops in his tracks and his body convulses violently. I don't stop. All the hate I have for him flows out of me.

He's the reason Emma's gone. He's the reason I became Fuse. He's the reason my world has completely changed.

Finally, with my energy spent, I drop to my knees and try to catch my breath. It feels like the wind's been knocked out of me. There's no way Bello survived that. I wonder if Dean survived. If Cale recognized him.

With the ringing in my ears, I don't hear the sirens until three police cars pull up right in front of the pump house. One of the officers spots me, and I force myself to my feet. Chancing another look back at them, I see Cale emerge from the building. He hesitates as the policemen point their guns at him. His eyes flicker up to me. I nod a thanks to him and he turns and races up the hill in the opposite direction. The police fire, but the bullets have no effect on his mutated body.

With a deep breath, I summon the last bit of energy I have and run.

CHAPTER NINETEEN

Mayor Banks among 14 Arrested for Mafia Involvement
By: Bebe Hawkins

Olympia Mayor Eugene Banks was among the 14 city employees arrested last night for their alleged involvement with organized crime leaders. In a statement released by the Olympia Police Department last night, documents indicating certain city officials who have been involved in crimes such as racketeering, forgery, fraud, slander, and other violations were presented to the police.

"It was a strong case," Police Chief Brian Barker said in a statement. "With it, we were able to confirm some of the information we had already gathered." Barker wouldn't reveal the name of the person who presented the documents, but he said it came from a "reliable source."

While the crimes listed cover a number of instances, some of the biggest and most recent acts are related to the redevelopment of the former Montgomery Works facility, specifically its environmental cleanup.

Fuse: Oblivion

"The initial document stating the site was properly cleaned up is completely false," Barker exclusively told the Tribune *during a follow-up interview early this morning. "The state has no record of ever sending someone out to review the area, and upon further inspection, it's very clear that the land is not ready for construction."*

Work on the project, which promised to create 140 low-income housing units, was postponed after developer Leon Wallace was killed by Fizz during the ground-breaking ceremony on March 10. Authorities are now saying it is likely that the project will not continue.

I fold up the paper and smile. Myra came through. Not that I had any doubts about that, but it's a relief now that it's out in the open. Too bad the article didn't mention that Cale was working on exposing the crooks behind the Works, but I don't think the *Tribune* would say anything about a potential exposé by a competing news outlet. Besides, it's not like Cale's research was completely useless. Myra looked over some of his notes to finish her case.

The important thing is, at least the story is out there. However he looks now, Cale made a difference. There won't be any families moving to the Works and getting sick from the toxic chemicals seeping up from the soil.

And with Martelli's contacts being arrested and eventually tried, there won't be any more developments like this one. That's the hope, at least.

Still, it's a shame Cale can't take credit for this. He worked so hard to expose this corruption, and essentially lost his life because of it. He deserved more. Everyone who became a victim of the Martelli family did.

"Well, he's all set to go as far as I'm concerned," Tucker breaks into my thoughts when he approaches.

We're at the Terry Lake Police Department. Even though they talked to him when he was taken from the shoot out to the hospital last week, they wanted to ask Dean more questions about what happened at the pump house. They're being extra thorough with him because of who his father is. I called Tucker as soon as I got away from the pump house last week. I couldn't let Dean get arrested for his father's actions.

I set the paper I was reading on the small table and stand up. "No charges filed or anything?"

He shakes his head. "No. Rizzoli—well, Albert Zalinski— vouched for Dean's innocence during it all."

"Yeah, I've been meaning to ask you about that all week. What's the deal with that? How long has Rizzoli been working with you guys?"

"He's been our mole for almost thirty years now. He's definitely a lifer. Very dedicated. Only the organized crime task force really knew that he was inside."

That would explain him sliding me the knife. But all of the evidence I found against him points to him being a criminal.

"I have so many questions."

He grins. "If you want, now that the Martelli empire is in shambles and he's officially retired, he might be open to talking with you guys. I'm sure you're worried about what this means for your company."

I nod, and try to play it off like that's my main concern. "Uh, right. Exactly."

Fishing in his breast pocket, he pulls out a sticky note. "Everything he used to communicate with the Martellis is evidence now, so he has a new number and everything. Here it is. Don't share that, though. I'm trusting you, Pierce."

"I won't." I take it from him. "Thanks, Tucker."

Patting me on the shoulder, Tucker smiles and says, "No problem, man. Take care of yourself. And stay out of trouble. I mean it this time."

"I'll try."

The clicking of crutches turns our attention down the hall where Dean approaches. His leg is wrapped and the crutches slow him down slightly, but otherwise he's himself.

"You ready to go?" I ask.

"Yeah, now that I'm officially a free man."

Luckily, the police came to the conclusion that Dean was a

pawn for Bello to draw out Martelli. Certainly looked that way, and with most of the witnesses dead because of Fizz, nobody is saying anything otherwise. We're definitely not going to tell them the real reason he was there. And, of course, there is Rizzoli's statement—or Zalinski, or whatever his name actually is. It's still too confusing.

"How's the leg?" Tucker asks Dean.

"Sore, but not too bad," he responds. "I'll be fine."

"Keep it elevated," Tucker adds.

"Yeah, we should probably get you home," I say.

———

THE CONDO IN midtown is now cordoned off for police investigation, so Dean and I are at the Stanley Hotel to meet with Rizzoli—Zalinski. It's going to take awhile to get used to that.

I called him right after we got home to set up a meeting with him. He was more than willing to explain everything. I know it's safe, but I can't help but feel anxious about going to meet with him. Especially with Dean on crutches.

The hotel building is just as beautiful inside as out, but I'm not paying much attention to it. My mind is too full of the questions I have for my boss—if he's even my boss anymore.

It's not until the elevator doors close shut that Dean and I break the silence we've held since we left the apartment.

"You nervous?" he asks.

"Yeah. You?"

He nods. "I don't know what I should ask him first."

I look down and study the design in the gold-plated floors. "Neither do I. But he helped us. He helped you. We should hear him out."

The elevator dings on the seventh floor and we step off, Dean lagging a little from his crutches. We meander down the narrow hallway to the end and knock on number 734.

I let out a quick breath and look to Dean once more. The man behind the door has been our enemy's ally for a long time. It's hard to change that perspective in my head.

Chapter Nineteen

When the door opens, the person I knew as Frank Rizzoli rests on his own set of crutches in front of me. Only, it's not quite the Rizzoli I remember. He's different, aside from the injury. First of all, he's smiling. I don't think I've ever seen him genuinely smile before. Second, he's dressed in a plain white T-shirt and black sweatpants. Quite the difference from the suits he always used to wear. And third, he's no longer clean-shaven. He has the starting of a beard.

"Gentlemen," he says, shaking hands with each of us, "come on in."

He has a full suite, and a swanky one at that. It's bigger than my apartment and has a full kitchen, living room, and a small dining table in the corner. Through two pocket doors I spot a king-sized bed and several shopping bags on the floor.

"Please forgive the way I'm dressed." He looks down at himself. "This is about the only thing I can wear that'll fit all of my bandages and everything comfortably. Not to mention, my clothes are still in my condo, which is closed off."

"It's okay," I tell him. Dean wore khaki shorts. It's still a little too chilly for them, but since we were coming to one of the ritziest hotels in the city, he wanted to look at least somewhat presentable.

"Have a seat," Zalinski says, shuffling over to the kitchen. "I can get you coffee or something."

"I can get it," I tell him. "You should sit. Both of you, actually."

Dean hops over to the couch and puts his leg up on the coffee table. He props his crutches against the edge of the couch.

Zalinski stays with me in the kitchen, pointing out where the coffee mugs are and all the additives before hopping over to sit on the other end of the couch.

I carry the three mugs over and take a seat in an open chair.

"Thank you, Mr. Pierce." Zalinski holds up his mug before taking a careful sip.

"So," Dean starts. I can tell he doesn't like that he's sitting closer to Zalinski than I am, but I'm the only one in this room who wasn't shot.

"So," Zalinski echoes.

"We have a lot of questions," I say.

He nods. "That's what you told me on the phone, yes. I understand. It has to be confusing. It is for me, and I lived through it."

"Detective Cross said you've been undercover for thirty years," I start.

He nods. "That's correct, yes." He points to Dean. "That was just before you were born."

Dean doesn't say anything. Doesn't even look at him. Just stares down at the steaming cup of coffee sitting on the table.

"Why don't you start from the beginning?" I suggest.

He rubs the scruff on his face and breathes in deeply. "That was a long time ago, as I've said. Actually, at that stage of my life, I was a lot like you are now, Mr. Pierce. I was twenty-two when I was hired by the Olympia Police Department as their IT specialist. Their technology was quite different then than it is today, let me assure you."

"Oh, so you're *actually* a tech person?" It's surprising to hear that the man I knew as Rizzoli wasn't completely a false identity.

"Yes. I told you some time ago that confidence avoids suspicion. It was better to play up the strengths I had than to develop new ones."

"So you weren't a cop?" I ask.

He shakes his head. "No, I wasn't."

"So how did you get to be their mole?"

"They were looking to get one of their own inside organized crime operations. Someone the crime families didn't know."

"Families?" I ask. Dean mentioned that there were multiple families before, but I've never heard the details of it.

"You have to understand, back then Carlo Martelli wasn't the only mob boss. There were two other families, all with connections as deep as Martelli has now—well, *had*." He looks over at Dean. "My condolences for your father."

To my surprise, Dean offers a tight smile and nod.

The damage Carlo Martelli sustained from Cale's attack wasn't fatal, but it might as well have been. Like the bodyguard protecting him—who was pronounced dead at the scene—Carlo's back was sprayed with acid, which did extensive damage to his spinal cord. His body is now completely paralyzed, although his brain is still very much alive.

Probably one of the worst punishments he could get is to live in a world without his influence. The same fate he served up to my brother a few months ago. Seems fitting.

"Anyway," Zalinski continues. "The task force at the time was most concerned with Martelli, which proved to be valid. He went to war with the other families and took over their self-mandated jurisdictions. It worked out well for me in my position, because at the time I was already an associate for the family. As Martelli's power grew throughout the city, so did his need for trustworthy men."

"And he trusted you?" I ask. "He didn't suspect you were with the police?"

"Carlo came to think of me as a friend."

"How did you manage that?"

"Well, keep in mind that I wasn't just thrown into the field. On the contrary, I went through mental and physical evaluations. It was almost a full year of training. They would've liked to have done more, but time was of the essence. It was important that I start young because Carlo would've been suspicious of someone older wanting to join."

"What about your life?" I ask. "Didn't you want to get married? Move on to other careers? Maybe even move away?"

"He did get married," Dean finally speaks up. "What was her name? Penelope, I think, right?"

Zalinski nods. "Yeah. That was real. Well, as real as I could have at the time. Which is what caused our divorce. I couldn't be completely honest with her about who I was, and she could tell. Not that it mattered, I suppose. She fell in love with the person I was pretending to be."

"But over thirty years, wasn't it harder to tell the difference between what was real and what wasn't?" I ask.

"Absolutely. It's why it's so strange to be able to talk about this now. For years it's been a closely kept secret that I swore to take to the grave if Martelli no longer trusted me."

"What about all the bad things you did?" Dean asks. "I remember you being the worst of the worst when I was younger."

"Despite what I led everyone to believe, I only killed three people in my life, and I've regretted each one. However, they were all out of my control."

I narrow my eyes and lean forward in the old wooden chair. "How did you manage that? If people thought of you as a killer, wasn't it because you *were*?"

"Well, there were different ways I avoided ending someone's life. I would contact the OPD and get the victim into witness protection. Not ideal, but at least they would be alive. And, unfortunately, there were times I had to have someone else do the deed for me. But understand the predicament I was in: if I was going to earn and maintain my place in the family in order to bring them down, I needed to convince them that I was this character I was playing."

"So you still killed," Dean says. "Even if you weren't technically the one pulling the trigger."

"Understand that killing was not something I enjoyed, and it was always a last resort that came only when my loyalty was questioned. And even then, I did my best to protect the victims. It worked with the both of you."

Dean and I look at each other and then back to Zalinski.

"What do you mean?" I ask.

"When did you protect me?" Dean adds.

"Mr. Adams, are you sitting in a jail cell right now? And Mr. Pierce, I've been protecting you from the moment Carlo took an interest in you. When he said he wanted to meet you, I volunteered to do it for him. That's why I sent Mr. Gotti to arrange a meeting with you under the pretense of giving you a job at Tranidek."

"So does that mean I'm unemployed now?"

Zalinski smiles and shakes his head. "No, it doesn't. The board of directors will have to select another CEO. Tranidek Energy will continue without me. Your job is safe."

I nod, relieved.

Chapter Nineteen

"As I stated in the letter I sent you while you were in the hospital, I looked into your history and saw that your skillsets aligned with the company and used that as my excuse to keep an eye on you," he explains. "Unfortunately, I wasn't able to protect Ms. Landry in the same way, although I tried."

I take a sip of my coffee. I don't like coffee, so it tastes bitter, but I need something to distract me from that time in my life. It doesn't seem like it was only six months ago.

"So how did you become the CEO *and* get so high up in Carlo's empire?" I ask to change the subject.

"Those in the family needed real jobs as a front to make money. James Alexander had restaurants, Michael Bello and Leon Wallace had their development companies, Luca Martelli had his position at the Midtown Trust Bank. Carlo knew that I was good with technology. He had connections at Tranidek. Back then, it wasn't the company that it is today. Robert Moyer wasn't even CEO, he was just a skilled technician who was very involved in the city and had many friends on city council."

"So he wanted you to keep an eye on Moyer?" Dean asks.

Zalinski nods. "Correct. Moyer liked me and I was good at my job, so I was promoted alongside him. When he became CEO, he kept me around as his assistant. When he passed—of natural causes, let me add—it made sense for me take his position since I had worked closely with him for so long."

"And the cops were okay with that?" I ask. "Wouldn't that distract you from the mission of bringing down the Martellis?"

"At first, I was merely supposed to be information on the inside. When there were still three crime families to watch, the task force put men in each of the other families. Unfortunately, they didn't succeed."

"They died?" I ask.

Zalinski nods again. "So I wanted to do all I could to keep up appearances. As long as I had an alibi for my whereabouts whenever Martelli questioned me—and served my purpose of being an influential person in the city—I was safe."

"Wow." I sit back in my chair. "This was a lot bigger than I thought."

Dean doesn't seem as convinced as I am. "What about Bello? Ethan overheard some people at Tranidek say that you and him were real close. Why would you befriend someone who ranked *lower* than you did in the family? How was that benefitting your mission?"

Zalinski stares at his half-empty coffee mug in his lap. "My friendship with Michael was genuine. Especially when I was married to Penelope. Our wives got along great together. I even helped Michael fund his development company when he was starting out."

"Why?" I ask.

"I thought it'd be good for the city. And a lot of his projects were. But the side businesses he also chose to operate to make extra money—the drugs, the prostitution, the thefts—no, Mr. Adams, I didn't agree with any of that."

"Is that why you stopped spending so much time with him?" I ask.

"Correct. Once Penelope left me, I had a better reason to distance myself from Michael. Still, I'm sure you can understand why it wasn't wise for me to completely cut him out of my life. Not with my mission for the OPD unfulfilled."

"What about Alexander?" Dean presses. "It's pretty obvious that you let him into my apartment so he could carve people up. Why'd you do that? How was that protecting me?"

He looks down. "Yes, I gave him a key. Again, my hands were tied. Plus, by then I knew you were staying with Mr. Pierce. I knew you were safe."

"How?" I ask.

Zalinski addresses me. "Mr. Adams here is an intelligent man who knows the way his father works." He looks over at Dean. "I knew the moment you suspected that you were being watched, you would find different living arrangements."

Dean studies him. I can almost see him trying to wrap his head around the real truth instead of the altered one we've believed for so long. Dean's whole life. "What about the body on my bike on Thanksgiving? That wasn't you, was it?"

"No. Regrettably, I was sent to investigate a suitable spot to hide a different body with Mr. Gotti." Zalinski meets my eyes. "Mr. Pierce, if I would've known we were looking for the grave of your brother, I would've done my best to warn you so you could better protect him. Please believe me when I say that I did all I could to protect him as well."

My throat goes dry and my stomach seems to hollow out. They were planning Cale's death that far in advance? While I was sitting on the patio chatting with my brother's attacker? I'm angry at Carlo, but most of all I feel guilty. As if I should've done something more for Cale.

"You were the one who sent the Black Hand letters, weren't you?" I ask.

He nods. "To your brother and Miss Connors."

"Oh." It's all I can say. The letter worked to save Myra, but only because I knew what had happened to Cale.

"It is my belief," Zalinski continues, "that Carlo's cousin Luca was the one who assisted Mr. Alexander with staging the body on Thanksgiving."

"Is that who let him on the roof of Tranidek Tower too?" I ask. "On my first day of work."

"I left for a business meeting at our facility on Ashland Avenue that afternoon. What I can only assume happened was that Mr. Gotti, who worked with me as my assistant at Tranidek, told Mr. Alexander about the roof access from the stairwell. My secretary never heard anything, and she says Mr. Gotti was in the office the whole time."

I stare at him, not wanting to believe him. It seems like he has an excuse for everything.

"How can we be sure that you're not lying to us now?"

Zalinski stretches forward with a grunt to set his mug down on the coffee table and sits back. "Mr. Pierce, I've done my best to protect you from the moment you witnessed that drive-by shooting with Miss Landry, especially once I figured out that you're Fuse."

This stops me cold. "What? How long have you known that?"

"At the dinner party, while everyone else seemed to be damning the man in black, you were touting his praise. Not only that, but you only seemed to show interest in Olympia's more concerning developments. After that, when Fuse seemed to interfere with Michael Bello's operations and your brother began to dig deeper into the Works, it confirmed my suspicions."

"What did my brother have to do with anything?" I ask. "He didn't know I was Fuse."

"I suppose I was wrong in that assumption, then. However, many of your assumptions about me have been proven wrong as well."

He's got a point there. I wonder how different things would be if I had known Rizzoli was with the police all along. But then, there were plenty of times that we were alone that he could've told me and he didn't. Martelli and his empire have been stopped, but at what cost?

"Don't worry," he says. "I'll keep your secret, even from the police."

"Thank you."

"I think I've given them more than enough information now, don't you?"

Dean smiles down into his coffee. "I guess so. You told them more than I ever have."

"You had to protect yourself, Mr. Adams. Look at the way your father reacted when he learned you broke omertà."

"Yeah," he mutters.

"So you're really not coming back to Tranidek?" I ask to change the subject.

"I don't believe so, no."

"So what does that mean?" Dean asks.

"I'm retiring. After thirty years of working undercover while also working my way to the top of one of the biggest companies in the city, I believe I deserve some time off, don't you?"

He's right. He did just give up basically his whole life. I've only given up the last six months of mine, and look at everything I've lost. I can't imagine all that he's lost in that time. Everything he's missed out on.

"Are there any more questions?" he asks.

"Too many to think of right now," Dean says.

"Well, you have my number. Please stay in touch."

"Mr., uh, Zalinski," I start.

He smiles. "Hearing that name again is going to take some getting used to."

"Well, I just wanted to say thank you for helping us."

"Yeah," Dean echoes.

"You're welcome," he says. "It was all a part of my job."

Chapter Twenty

When we get home, I help Dean get situated on the couch. Once his leg is propped up, I get to work in the kitchen.

"I'm making *you* a meal for a change," I tell him proudly.

"It's not going to put me back in the hospital, is it?"

"Very funny, but I actually know how to cook. Not as well as you can, but I'm not an idiot. How's brinner sound?"

"Brinner?" he asks.

"Breakfast for dinner?" I ask as I pull a carton of eggs out of the fridge. "Tell me you've heard of it before."

He laughs and puts his hands up. "Hey, whatever you want. I won't turn down a free meal."

I crack the eggs onto a pan. "It's weird that Rizzoli was working with the police all this time, isn't it?"

He rolls his head from side to side as he lets out a heavy sigh. "Ethan, I'd rather not talk about it right now. I've known Rizzoli my whole life—well, I thought I did. I just found out that I don't really know him at all. It's going to take some time to process."

"Right, sorry."

"Don't worry about it. Let's just talk about something else."

"Any news about your father?" I ask.

"No, he's still the same. They're going to bring in a specialist, but he'll probably have to go to a long-term facility."

"Huh," I say in reply.

Dean hasn't said too much about what he thinks of his father's injury. Or his betrayal. He doesn't seem upset about it, but I'm sure a part of him still wants his father to be free. Still wishes the bond they had been forming was genuine. It's human nature.

"Yeah," Dean continues, "but I guess the good part is that no one will assume I'm working with him again."

I turn off the stove and the sausage continues to sizzle on the skillet. Pulling out two plates from the cupboard, I say, "No, but his surviving lackeys might come to you for leadership. Or revenge."

"That's why I have you. To zap anyone who tries to kill me." He smirks. "But I doubt that anyone would come to me for leadership."

I carry our plates to the couch and hand Dean his. I lift his injured leg over my lap, but he still cringes. "Sorry."

"Everything's just really tender," he says. "You don't realize how much you use that muscle until it's ripped apart."

"True." I stab my fork into my food.

"I start physical therapy next week."

"That's funny."

He takes a bite and mutters, "The irony is not lost on me. The doctor wants to give it a little more time to heal before I start using it. You should be careful, though."

"Why's that?"

"Well when you went to PT, you took your therapist home."

I blush and look down at my food. "I don't think I have anything to worry about."

We're quiet as we eat. The only sound is our silverware clinking on our plates.

"So…we're good, right?"

He narrows his eyes. "What do you mean?"

"Like, this is an actual thing?" I wave my hand between us.

"We're really doing this? We're really together?"

He smiles. "Yes, Ethan."

"And you're sure you're ready?"

He rocks his head back and forth again. "For the most part, yeah. What happened is something I'll have to live with for the rest of my life. I'll get there. With your help. Are you sure you're okay with it?"

I tap my fork against my plate as I stare out the window. A few months ago I wouldn't have believed this would be my life. The idea might've even been revolting. Now that I've lost a lot of people close to me, I've realized that it's important to hold on to them as much as I can.

"Yeah. I mean, it's still weird and new and a little uncomfortable, but this is where I want to be." I reach for his hand. "Right here with you."

He flashes me a cheesy grin. "Aww!"

"Okay, okay, okay."

My phone buzzes in my pocket and I pull my hand away from Dean's. Stretching to reach for it—while trying not to hurt Dean any more—I manage to answer just before it cuts to voice-mail.

"Hello?"

"Ethan, hey." It's Myra. "How's Dean doing?"

"He's good. He's home now. Just needs to heal and then it's on to physical therapy."

"That's good. Yeah, glad to hear it… So is, uh, everything okay with…everything else?"

My eyebrows scrunch together. "Like what?"

"Like…" She laughs nervously. "I can't believe I'm saying this, but he's not being arrested or anything, is he?"

Suddenly she's not the only one bursting with nervous laughter. "No, he's not. He went in for some final questions this morning, but Tucker says he's all set."

"Good. That's good."

"Yeah."

Silence. Neither of us know quite what to say. I don't want to assume a friendship if she's still having trouble processing my confessions—both Fuse and Dean. I'm sure on her end she's wondering what she can ask so she doesn't offend me. Instead, I bring up the one person I know we both have in common.

"Hey, I need to talk to you about Cale."

Dean looks up at me with surprise, but I ignore him.

"What about him?" Myra asks quickly. "Did you find any new leads?"

I take a deep breath. "Well, sort of. I know where he is. Rather, *what* he is."

The excitement seems to drain from her voice. "What do you mean?"

"Cale's research into the Works got him into some hot water," I start. "With the Martellis, mostly."

She scoffs. "We figured that. What did—what happened? Is he alive? Is he okay?"

Now I kind of regret bringing this up. Missing him and wondering if he'll ever come home was hard enough, but will she be any better knowing what he's become? Knowing that there's no way he'll ever be who he was before? She doesn't need another thing to worry about. But she has a right to know what happened to him. She needs to be able to move on.

"They threw him in a chemical pit at the Works. They thought it'd kill him, and it should have." I pause. "But it didn't."

"What do you mean it didn't?"

"You know that guy who attacked Leon Wallace at the ground breaking for the Works? Fizz, they're calling him. Myra, that's Cale."

I wait for her response, but all she says is, "Oh."

"Yeah. His body mutated when it was exposed to the chemicals. He's alive but…he's not the same. Physically, at least."

"Oh," she repeats. "And you're sure of this because…with your…because of Fuse?"

"Yeah."

"Did he talk to you? Is he dangerous? Did he mean to kill those people?"

"I don't know. He didn't kill us, so I'm sure he's still in there somewhere," I say.

"Then maybe there's a way to fix him. Bring him back so he's norm—"

"Myra, there isn't a cure for this."

"How can you be sure?"

"Because once he's mutated, he can't be put back. It doesn't work that way, I guess."

"But we have to try."

"And how much pain would he go through while we tested out this theory? We have to accept the fact that Cale's gone."

I hear her cry on the other end. I really wish I would've told her all of this in person.

"We were right, though. Cale's not dead."

She scoffs.

"Listen, even though he was attacking people at the Works, he stopped when he saw us. That means a part of him is still alive."

"Maybe."

"I don't really know what's going to happen now that the Martelli family has imploded. Cale's enemies are gone and—"

"I want to see him."

"Myra, I'm not sure if—"

"You said it yourself: a part of him is still alive. That means he remembers us. I have to know. I can't just keep wondering. Even if it's a good-bye, I need to do this to move forward."

I don't know what the right answer is here. It's not like Cale's dead. For all intents and purposes, he's alive. But he's not the same. Separating that in our minds will be harder than it seems. I've tried, and still a part of me hopes that there'll be a cure for his disfigurement.

But if Myra's willing to move on, then I should too.

"Okay. Let's go."

———

SLEET PELTING THE ground has left an icy coating over everything by time we get to the Works. It's now fenced off to keep everyone out. A perfect hideout for a mutant in such an urban location.

Chapter Twenty

The place where Dean and I came through the last time we were here is fenced off now. Myra and I had to find another spot in the fence where the chain links weren't fully secured to the metal supports, so we were able to push through and get inside before anyone saw us.

The security cameras haven't been installed yet, but they're coming. Myra says the city is even considering tearing down what's left of the Works. First they need to put their council back together, though.

"This place is creepy," Myra pulls her jacket tighter and shivers as we step into a cavernous warehouse. Cale wasn't in the office with the clippings, and I didn't want to make him feel like he was cornered, so we kept our distance, opting to call for him throughout the empty buildings.

The sound of the sleet hitting the windows and the faint drip of a leaky roof are the only noises that fill the damp space between our calls.

"No arguments here."

We search through two of the buildings before we hear something in the third. A low grumble echoes throughout the cavernous space.

"Cale?" I call out.

The grumbling stops.

"Cale, sweetie, it's Myra and Ethan," she says.

Still nothing.

"Ethan told me what happened," she continues. "I just want to see you. To make sure you're okay. Please come out."

Just when I'm sure we're talking to no one, a blue tarp crinkles across the room. Myra steps back and reaches for my arm, her other hand over her mouth.

Through his sagging face, Cale watches us carefully as he slowly steps into view. When he's only twenty feet away, Myra takes a careful step toward him.

"Oh, Cale." Her voice breaks. "Look what they've done to you."

He looks down, shameful.

"We got them," I tell him. "Martelli's paralyzed and…I killed

Bello." I try to ignore the surprise in Myra's face. "We put the rest of the bastards away because of the work you did on this place."

He looks up at me, and I think I can see the hint of a smile through the skin rolls.

"Cale, I don't know how much you remember from before, but I hope you never forget how much I love you." Myra sniffles. "It's going to be really hard to move on from you. Everything we had planned. That future together is just a dream now. I don't know where my life is going anymore." She wipes at her face with her sleeve. "I know if you could, you would be with me."

He nods and looks between us with sad eyes. Cale is in there. And he does remember. Myra's right. If it were up to him, he'd be back at home with us. Not lurking in a dank old warehouse that's awaiting demolition. He deserves better than this.

But there's nothing we can do about it. What's done is done, and the people who are responsible for turning him into this are either dead or incarcerated. As it should be. It still doesn't make me feel any better, though.

I've considered asking Cale if he'd be willing to help me during my Fuse outings, but I don't want to bring it up now in front of Myra. The relationship she had with him is gone and there isn't any way she can salvage it now that he's Fuse. Not only that, but I can't imagine the pain Cale's going through knowing that he can't be with the woman he loves. It's better for both of them to just move on.

After we've all had time to adjust to the idea, I'll see if my brother is interested in joining forces with me. I know I'd love it. Continuing any sort of relationship with him is better than nothing, even if it's not quite the same as when he was my roommate.

Myra approaches him and reaches for his arm. "Good-bye Cale. I love you. I always will." She meets his eyes and lingers a moment before turning and quickly walking out of the building.

I follow her, but linger by the doorway and look back at him. "Good-bye for now, Cale."

Behind the Book: FUSE: OBLIVION

Thanks so much for reading! I hope you enjoyed the book and the series as a whole. After having the idea bouncing around in my head for two years before I even started writing *Origin*, it's weird to be on the other side of the whole series.

This book has been possibly the hardest book of the three to write. When I was first plotting out release dates, I figured I could push this book a little closer because hey, it's the third book, I'll be writing in an established world, how long can it really take to write?

Yeah, I was dead wrong about that, for a number of reasons.

First, I wasn't positive how exactly I wanted to write this book because I wanted to keep this trilogy open-ended in case I want to write more Fuse books in the future. (I don't have anything planned, but I'm not ruling it out.) So figuring out the storyline for how to wrap up the major story arc of the Martelli family was the first obstacle.

Second, I was so focused on writing the first draft and getting it done in between drafts of *Omertà* that I left out A LOT of

187

details in the first draft, which came in at just over 31,000 words (for reference, the finished book is 58,000 words). I was determined not to do what I call "lazy editing" for this book, so it took me longer to do the second draft because I was rewriting a lot of it and adding in so many new scenes.

Actually, the idea of Rizzoli being an informant for the police—hopefully one of the biggest plot twists of the series—didn't come to me until halfway through the third draft, just before I sent it to my editor. It all just clicked in my head and I remembered that I mentioned in the *Origin* that the police had an informant and Rizzoli became that. (In the first draft of the book, Rizzoli died at the end of the book in the pump house.) I went through every scene throughout the series with him in it to see how I could explain away some of his actions and Chapter 19 basically wrote itself. I think it worked out nicely, but I'm probably biased.

Two other "deleted scenes" were actually flashback chapters that showed some of the highlights of what happened in the four months between *Omertà* and *Oblivion*. There was a scene at Christmas time where Dean gets uninvited to his father's for the holidays and so spends it with Ethan and another where Myra wins the election and they celebrate. But it was confusing for the linear storyline to throw them in since I hadn't used flashbacks in this series before. So they got deleted pretty quickly in the fourth draft and those details were worked in elsewhere in the book.

I also decided to tone down the LGBT theme in this book, not because it's a topic that shouldn't be discussed, but because it was always my intention to have Ethan and Dean's romantic relationship be an "Oh, by the way..." instead of a major focal point. It kind of got away from me in *Omertà*, but Ethan needed to deal with all those feelings and then everything that happened between Dean and James Alexander...

Anyway, with this book, I realized that I need to give myself about four months to write a full-length novel like this. Especially one with so many layers and twists and turns. (Note to self: ORGANIZE TWISTS BETTER.) I ended up finishing this book

Behind the Book

TEN DAYS before it's release date. Yeah, I was biting my nails a little bit, but this book was so complicated.

Part of the reason the fourth draft took me so long was because my editor was asking me a bunch of "what if" questions about the plot and I was having a hard time remembering some of the details I thought were implied. I powered through it, but it definitely made me realize that I need to plot in a different way in the future.

I don't have any immediate plans to continue this series (as of March 2018…), but I'm not closing myself off to the idea. The only trouble is, I'll have to come up with a whole new story arc, which would mean another trilogy, so it's a bigger commitment than "just one more book."

What I DO have plans for is a second superhero series, tentatively called "Heat." It will (hopefully) be a little lighter than Fuse in terms of subject matter (maybe some of the characters will actually laugh once in a while…), but it'll still be just as action-filled and mysterious. That's the plan, at least. Not sure when exactly that series is coming, but I'm thinking Spring 2019.

Thanks again for reading! Please leave a review on the retailer you bought it from or on Goodreads. Don't forget to follow me on social media and check out the rest of my books at DavidNethBooks.com/Books. If you want to get in touch with me, visit DavidNethBooks.com/About.

Thanks again!

DavidNethBooks.com/Newsletter

Kathy and her sister, Samantha, have always been a team. Throughout their time as witches, they've taken out more than their share of bad guys. But after Kathy meets Will, who she learns is a demonic Dark Knight, her loyalties begin to change.

Meanwhile, Samantha doesn't trust Will or his intentions. Still, Kathy can't help but feel tempted by the dark side as she falls deeper in love with Will. Crossing over would give Kathy the freedom to do whatever she wanted with her magic. No rules. No limitations. It would also mean breaking the bond she has always shared with her sister, who has made it clear that she wants nothing to do with the dark side.

When Will proposes they take over the underworld, Kathy loves the idea of having power. But it also leaves her with a choice that will change her life: abandon her family and the life she has always known, or give up the love of her life forever.

———

Available in ebook, paperback, and audio!
DavidNethBooks.com/TheFullMoon

More by the Author

To find the rest of the author's books visit
DavidNethBooks.com/Books

———

Subscribe to his newsletter to be the first to know of new releases and special deals!
DavidNethBooks.com/Newsletter

———

If you enjoyed the book, please consider leaving a review on Goodreads or the retailer you bought it from. Reviews help potential readers determine whether they'll enjoy a book, so any comments on what you thought of the story would be very helpful!

About the Author

David Neth is the author of the Fuse series, the Small Town Christmas series, the Under the Moon series, and other stories. He lives in Batavia, NY, where he dreams of a successful publishing career and opening his own bookstore.

———

Follow the author at

www.DavidNethBooks.com
www.facebook.com/DavidNethBooks
www.twitter.com/DavidNethBooks
www.instagram.com/dneth13

www.ingramcontent.com/pod-product-compliance
Lightning Source LLC
Chambersburg PA
CBHW032004180726

48283CB00008B/2559